MARIE FERRARELLA

The Doctor's Guardian

ROMANTIC

SUSPENSE

Recycling programs
for this product may
not exist in your area.

ISBN-13: 978-0-373-27745-2

THE DOCTOR'S GUARDIAN

Copyright © 2011 by Marie Rydzynski-Ferrarella

Books by Marie Ferrarella

MARIE FERRARELLA

This *USA TODAY* bestselling and RITA® Award—winning author has written more than two hundred books for Harlequin Books and Silhouette Books, some under the name Marie Nicole. Her romances are beloved by fans worldwide. Visit her website at www.marieferrarella.com.

To Kathleen Creighton,
with deepest sympathies.
The heart recovers,
even when we don't want it to.

Chapter 1

She didn't have time for this.

Doctor—she adored the sound of that—Veronika Pulaski, "Nika" to her family and friends, was one of those people who'd been born making lists. Tons of lists. *Different* lists that were applicable to nearly every aspect of her incredibly fast-paced life. Long lists that helped keep her on track.

Nowhere, not even remotely, on today's extra long list was the entry: get stuck in the hospital elevator this morning.

Yet here she was.

Stuck.

And getting more frustrated by the minute.

There hadn't been anyone riding up with her when the elevator car—which was definitely in need of renovations—had come to an abrupt, teeth-jarring halt in between floors. Consequently, there was no one to talk to, no one to help take her mind off the predicament, at least for a few minutes. There wasn't even annoyingly distracting piped-in music that her cousins had told her there once had been.

Nothing but the ticking of the clock in her head as it waved goodbye to the minutes that were tumbling away one by one. Minutes that she was supposed to be spending in the Geriatrics Unit.

This was actually supposed to be her day off. Her *first* day off in a little more than two incredibly busy, exhausting weeks. But she had opted to come in. *No good deed went unpunished,* she thought as she stood there, willing the elevator back to life. It remained frozen in place.

So much for a career in telekinesis.

The hospital's Pediatric and Geriatric Units were desperately short staffed. They were that way not because the missing staff members were sick, but because they could *potentially* be sick.

The problem was a new strain of flu that was currently making the rounds, a particularly resilient strain that had already taken quite a toll on the population since its appearance on the scene nearly a month ago, cutting down far more people than was usual in these cases. The vaccine that had been created to prevent it had only met with marginal success. And, as usual, the very young and the very old were particularly susceptible to the illness.

The fear was that any of the staff who hadn't contracted the flu yet might be on the verge of coming down with it, or could be, at the very least, unwitting carriers. As a result, only those staff members who had already had the flu—dubbed the Doomsday Flu by some supremely insensitive, brain-dead media reporter because of the number of deaths associated with it in a short period of time—were allowed to work in either Pediatrics or Geriatrics.

As luck would have it, she was one of them.

Nika had come down with a rip-roaring case of the flu before any statistics had even been available about the disease. When it had suddenly caused her knees to buckle and her head to spin, sending her falling into her bed, Nika had been miserable, but she really hadn't thought anything about it. This, to her, was all part of being a doctor who dealt with an entire range of patients every day.

As it turned out, she'd contracted it from one of the patients in the Geriatric Unit. That patient had passed away a little more than twenty-four hours after being admitted into Patience Memorial. But Nika, incredibly healthy and in better than ordinary physical condition, was back on her feet five days after she became ill and back at work in seven.

Her return had almost been hailed with rose petals scattered in her path. Doctor Jorgensen, the head of the Geriatrics Unit, was that happy and that relieved to see her.

"You have no idea how shorthanded we are," the tall, gaunt specialist told her.

Nika might not have had an inkling then, but she quickly became educated by the end of the first grueling day. The unit was extremely short staffed across the board, and that meant doctors, nurses and even orderlies were in limited supply. Those who were there were stretched almost beyond their endurance level.

Trial by fire, Nika had thought at the time. And

that was fine with her. She didn't mind working hard. Practicing medicine—helping patients, especially senior patients—was what it was all about to her.

What she minded terribly was being stuck in an elevator when she had patients waiting for her. She absolutely *hated* wasting time and that was what she was being forced to do.

She'd reported an emergency on the dedicated line and pressed the alarm the second it became clear that the elevator wasn't experiencing a momentary hiccup or temporary glitch in its system but a paralyzing malfunction. One that, left unchecked, could go on indefinitely.

She and her mounting claustrophobia didn't have "indefinitely."

Besides, the shrilled alarm was *really* beginning to get on her nerves. How long could a person go on listening to that kind of loud noise and not go deaf—or slightly crazy? She had no desire to be a test case.

Nika gave it all of almost five minutes and then, with a frustrated, edgy sigh, she picked up the dedicated line and waited for someone to come on the other end of the phone again.

When she heard the line being picked up, she didn't even wait for them to say anything. Instead, she jumped right in.

"Hello, this is Dr. Veronika Pulaski again. How much longer is it going to be before someone fixes the elevator?" she asked.

"Three minutes less than when you asked the last time," the weary voice on the other end of the call told her. A little more sympathy was evident as the man went on. "Look, I understand your frustration, but the maintenance guy's out sick with the flu—"

Nika rolled her eyes. Someone else down with the flu. She was really beginning to hate that word. "And there's no one else around to fix this? The hospital's got eight elevators—you can't tell me that there's only one maintenance guy."

She heard another huge sigh. "Yes, I can, Doctor. Cutbacks," the man explained before she could challenge him on the information. "We're trying to get someone from the elevator company to come out but it might be a while."

Terrific. "Define 'a while,'" Nika requested through clenched teeth.

"Not quick," was all the weary voice on the other end of the line said.

Superterrific. "Could you at least shut down the alarm?" Nika asked. "I'm going deaf down here."

"That," the man told her, brightening a little, "I can do." Even as he said it, the alarm suddenly stopped blaring. The sound, though, continued to echo in Nika's head like a phantom bell ringer who had come to life and now refused to die.

"Thank you!" Realizing that she was still shouting to be heard over an alarm that was no longer actually sounding, Nika lowered her voice and repeated, "Thank you."

"Yeah, don't mention it. I'll ring you when the guy gets here," the man promised.

"Please," Nika underscored.

But she was talking to a dead line. Annoyed, frustrated, she replaced the receiver in the small, silver space where it ordinarily resided. She left the little cubbyhole door open.

Because there was nothing else she could do, Nika leaned against the elevator wall and slid down onto the floor, resigned to wait for the appearance of the elusive elevator repair man.

Or Armageddon, whichever came first.

"You're going to be okay, G," Detective Cole Baker told the woman who was sitting up in the hospital bed, her small hand holding on to his.

Or maybe he was holding on to hers. At this point, he really couldn't have said with any certainty just who was reassuring whom. What he did know was that being here, in the hospital, with his eighty-four-year-old grandmother made him incredibly and uncomfortably restless.

Cole was accustomed to being around the woman in a completely different setting. One that was filled with energy and action. He was used to seeing his almost athletically trim grandmother bustling about her two-story home, the home she'd taken him into when one tragedy after another had left him homeless, wounded and orphaned.

Ericka Baker had been sixty-seven at the time, a feisty, vital widow preparing to move into a condo with her then-boyfriend, Howie. After a lifetime of hard work, she'd been planning on enjoying herself for a change.

However, the second she'd heard what had happened to him, his grandmother terminated the sale of her house and opened her home and her arms to Cole. Never once in all the seventeen years that followed had she made him feel that he was the reason her boyfriend had left, or that he was a burden.

She'd made him feel, instead, like a prize she'd been awarded in the second half of her life. The second half of her life because Ericka Baker fully expected to live way past a hundred. She'd told him that more than once.

To that end, his grandmother religiously went to yoga classes and watched everything that went into her mouth, referring to it as "fuel" rather than "food."

Despite her own eating habits, she'd periodically made him cookies. Other times she had the occasional pizza delivered for his enjoyment. She'd encouraged him to be his own person, find his own path.

Throughout what was left of his childhood and then adolescence, Ericka Baker had been an outstanding, dynamic creature—the one constant in his life. The one person he knew he could always come to with anything if he needed to.

She'd wanted him to become a lawyer, like his grandfather had been. But when he joined the police force, there'd been no one prouder or more supportive than his grandmother. He had the feeling, deep down, that his grandmother would have been just as supportive of him if he'd decided to be a beekeeper or a musician. She was supportive of *him,* the person, not some ongoing plan. For that very reason, he'd allowed himself to love her even while he successfully shut out the rest of the world.

Oh, he functioned and interacted and was the best possible policeman and then police detective that he could be. But he let no one into his inner sanctum. No one had access past the barriers he'd erected long ago. He didn't want to care about anyone, except for his grandmother.

Cole had lost his father to a roadside bomb in a

foreign country, his only brother to a car-versus-bicycle hit-and-run accident, and his mother to a bullet she'd put in her own head—after shooting one at him. Her attempt at a murder/suicide had just missed its mark, but not the lesson that came with it.

All that, especially the last, had forever changed him.

When Cole grew older, he began to understand that his mother's grief was just too great for her to handle and that she'd shot at him because she hadn't wanted him to be left behind to face the world on his own.

But the bullet she'd fired at him had bypassed all his vital organs and he had lived, even as she had died. Lived, once he had come out of his coma, with an incredible emptiness and a lack of desire to continue living in this cruel existence that had deprived him of everyone he loved.

That was when he discovered that his grandmother—his father's mother—had entered his life. She'd flown in from New York to be by his bedside, which was where she'd remained, keeping vigil, until he came out of his coma, both the literal one and then the self-imposed, emotional one that followed.

She'd embraced him, wept over him and then informed him that they would both move on. She made sure that he knew that there was no other option left to him.

In a strange sort of way, his grandmother gave him life. Again. And while he kept the rest of the world at arm's length, he would have literally given up that life that she'd restored for him years ago in an instant for her without being asked.

It pained Cole to see his grandmother like this. To see her looking so fragile, so pale and all but fading against the white sheets. Lying there, Ericka Baker seemed somehow smaller, even though she wasn't exactly a large woman by any standard of measurement other than an emotional one.

But G, as she'd instructed him to call her—she hated being referred to as Grandmother, saying it made her feel old—had, in the last few years, developed a heart condition: atrial fibrillation. He'd found out about it quite by accident. In the neighborhood, he'd stopped by for a surprise visit and found her medication on the kitchen counter. She'd forgotten to put it away. Added to that, there were times when she just seemed to drift away, sometimes even right in the middle of a conversation with him.

It wasn't because she was preoccupied, the way he'd first hoped. She just seemed to be mentally "away." After conferring with her primary care physician he finally had to admit to himself she was developing Alzheimer's. Alzheimer's, that dreaded disease that ultimately robbed a person of their identity, while the family lost a loved one years before death put in the ultimate claim for them.

But this morning, thank God, the woman's blue eyes weren't vacant, they were vividly alive, taking in everything. His grandmother was here, with him, and not overly happy about the location she found herself in. Hospitals, she'd always maintained, were for sick people and she never thought of herself as falling into that category.

"Of course I'm going to be all right, Coleman," she declared firmly. She knew she had no choice—she needed to have this procedure done to finally put an end to those heart palpitations that she'd been putting up with, the ones that had become all but disabling. "We just need to get this damn thing over with," she added. "Where's that doctor they said was coming? The one they promised was going to be here—" she paused to look at the clock on the wall, its numbers purposely oversized to accommodate the patients on this part of the floor "—ten minutes ago?"

It was getting late and he needed to get going. But not before he had a few words with the doctor who, for the most part, would be taking care of his grandmother. G was far too precious a human being for him to leave her welfare in the hands of an unknown stranger.

"I'll go find out what's keeping him," Cole volunteered.

But Ericka's fingers, still strong, tightened around his hand, keeping him in place. "You're going to be late for work," Ericka insisted.

She didn't like being the cause of that. She'd already told him more than once that she was perfectly capable of getting to the hospital by herself and handling her own admission, but he wouldn't hear of it. He insisted on coming with her.

Cole was such a good boy, she thought, but she couldn't be selfish with him. He had a life that went beyond her and she needed him to remember that, just in case…

Well, just in case, she told herself, letting the thought go unfinished.

Cole looked at his grandmother. His mouth curved in an affectionate smile.

"Work'll keep, G. I took a few personal hours off and I'm not leaving until I get to talk to this doctor, who doesn't seem to have any sense of time," he said, ending in a somewhat irritated note.

Cole glanced over his shoulder at the door that wasn't opening to admit anyone. Nothing got to him more than those who thought their time was more valuable than the people they dealt with.

"I'll be right back," he promised, taking his grandmother's hand off his own and gently laying it down on top of her bedclothes.

Striding toward the nurses' station in the middle of the floor, Cole found only one harried-looking nurse manning the area.

As he approached, one of the phones started ringing. He swallowed a curse as the woman picked up the receiver before he got to her.

"Geriatrics Unit. This is Estelle," she said in a somewhat hoarse voice.

Masking an exasperated sigh, Cole tried to look patient as he stood on the other side of the desk and waited for the woman to be finished. Judging by the put-upon, distressed look on her face, this was not a personal call. The dialogue bore out his assumption.

"Yes, as soon as I can. Really. No. If you could just send me someone to help out over here, I—hello? Hello?"

With a deep sigh, she hung up the phone, looking even worse for wear.

The second the nurse removed the receiver from her ear, Cole stepped up to lay claim to her attention. "Excuse me, my grandmother's in room 412. We've been waiting for the last two hours for some mythical doctor to materialize. Just how much longer is she supposed to wait for this doctor?" he asked with as much restraint as he could muster.

"Who's your grandmother?" the woman asked, her voice strained.

"Ericka Baker. She's in room 412," he repeated, struggling to rein in his impatience. "I'm Detective Cole Baker with the NYPD and I want to talk to whoever they've assigned to her case before I leave," he told her gruffly. "I don't think that's too much to ask. Now where the hell is he?"

The nurse, he noticed as he grew progressively more irritated, looked uncomfortable. Why? Was she about to snow him, saying something about how busy this missing doctor was or something equally as unacceptable?

"Stuck," the nurse responded.

"Stuck where? In some paper-pushing meeting?" he asked contemptuously. He was ready either to demand another doctor or ask where the meeting was so that he could go there and speak with this so-called "really excellent physician" as his grandmother's doctor had called this person. And then carry the man back if need be.

"No, in an elevator," Estelle corrected. "Maintenance just called to tell me that *she* had set off an alarm because she was stuck in an elevator."

So that was what all the noise earlier had been about. Why wasn't anyone doing anything about it? "Get her unstuck."

Estelle shook her head. "Not that simple. They just told me that they can't get a repairman here for at least another hour. Maybe more." The answer, she could see, was not the one he wanted. "Between the flu and cutbacks, it's like the whole world is shorthanded," she explained, obviously far from happy about the state of affairs herself.

Another hour spent waiting was unacceptable. Especially the "maybe more" part. There had to be something that could be done. It took him less than a minute to think about it. Cole was accustomed to taking matters into his own hands. G had raised him that way.

"Where's the elevator now?" he asked.

"They said it's stuck between the third and fourth floor."

"Show me which one it is," he instructed. There was no room for argument.

Estelle looked at the police detective uncertainly. Then, compelled by the no-nonsense expression on his face, she rose to her feet. She didn't have to be told that this was not a man people said no to.

"This way."

It surprised Nika how fast the temperature could rise within the enclosed elevator car. She'd already taken off her lab coat and unbuttoned her blouse as far as she could and still remain decent for the repairman when—and if—he showed up.

She was grateful that she wasn't overly claustrophobic, but this little incident could definitely send her in that direction. Growing increasingly restless, Nika raised her eyes to the ceiling. In between the two waning fluorescent lights there was what looked to be a trapdoor.

Was it a way out?

Not that it did her any good, she thought darkly. She had nothing to stand on in order to access it. Not even if she stood up on her toes. At her tallest, she measured five foot six, the ceiling was at least a good foot and a half above her, if not more.

Nika continued looking up at the trapdoor. That *had* to be what it was. What other use could it have? If she jumped up, she thought, rising to her feet, she just might be able to push it open—provided the door wasn't bolted down.

Of course it was bolted down, she silently argued, mocking herself. Why wouldn't it be?

But then, she'd just seen a memo that said the elevators were scheduled to be renovated in another month. The rest of the hospital had already gone through a makeover, but the elevators had been left out of the last two updates. Consequently, they were all incredibly old-fashioned. Maybe the bolts or screws or whatever it was that held that section of the ceiling in place were weak, ready to break.

At the very least, even if she couldn't get out, if she jarred the trapdoor open she'd be able to get some air into the stifling elevator car.

The promise of that was all the motivation she needed.

Bracing herself, Nika jumped up, her hand outstretched above her head. Missing contact, she jumped again. And then a third time, managing to stretch her fingers up a little farther each time.

On her fourth jump, she screamed. Half in triumph and half in stunned amazement.

The section she was trying to move moved all right. All the way off.

The next second, there was a man hanging upside down in the immobilized elevator car. His dark brown hair flowed away from a chiseled, hard-looking face. It was the kind of expression that inspired instant obedience. Oddly enough, she wasn't afraid.

"Give me your hand," he ordered gruffly.

The words, *Come with me if you want to live,* echoed mockingly in her brain.

This was no time to recall movie trivia, Nika upbraided herself. And yet, there it was.

Because this definitely felt like a scene out of some old action movie.

Chapter 2

Nika snapped out of her semi-dazed state a moment later. "What?" she cried.

She was fairly certain that an elevator repairman would have been trying to do something with the cable's mechanisms in a far more stable, accessible place, rather than lowering himself into the stalled elevator car like a frustrated trapeze artist trying to make a dramatic comeback.

Blood rushed to Cole's head. This was not exactly an ideal position to be in and definitely not something he would have chosen to do if there was any other way to go. But according to the nurse he'd talked to on his grandmother's floor, the company that handled maintaining the elevators wouldn't have a repairman out for at least another hour. That was completely unacceptable to him. He needed to speed things along and this was the only way open to him: rescuing the trapped doctor.

Stretching his hand out toward the stunned blonde looking up at him, his legs securely wrapped around the cable, which was most likely permanently staining his gray slacks with grease, Cole could only reach down so far. She would have to make up the difference. "I said, give me your hand."

He had to be kidding, right? "Who *are* you?"

"The tooth fairy," Cole growled.

He was in no mood for twenty questions. He wasn't sure just how much longer he could hang down like this. Each second that passed by made it that much harder. The hastily conceived plan was to pull her up out of the elevator car and get her to stand on top of it. From there, he was fairly sure he could get her out to the fourth floor. Fortunately, the elevator had gotten stuck closer to the fourth floor, rather than right in between the two floors. Every little inch helped.

"Now give me your damn hand," he demanded. "Unless you want to stay inside this box until that mythical repairman turns up."

He had a very persuasive argument. There was no way she wanted to stay here a moment longer.

"No!" Nika cried.

She stretched first both hands up, and then leaned into stretching just one. That got her a tiny bit closer, but she still couldn't reach him. Standing on her toes didn't help. It was a matter of "almost, but not quite."

Frustration raked over her, making her thin blouse stick to her skin as perspiration slipped over her. Dropping her hands to her sides, she looked up at him.

"How...?"

He anticipated her question. Extending his hands

down as far as he could, he ordered, "Jump up! I'll grab your arms."

Another question occurred to her but Nika bit it back. There was no point in showering him with queries. Anxious to leave her confinement, she would have been willing to jump up and grab hold of the devil himself if he'd just get her out of here. Even with him hanging upside down, she could tell that this handsome, although unsmiling and gruff, man wasn't the devil.

At least, not exactly.

Whatever else this man might be as he went about his life, right now, at this moment, this Flying Wallenda wannabe was the answer to her prayers.

Nika squared her shoulders. "Ready?" she asked him, bracing herself.

There was more than a shade of impatience in his stony face. Nika could recognize it even upside down. "Lady—"

"You're ready," she pronounced. Blowing out a breath, she gave it her all and sprang up as high as she could, her hands reaching up for the sky.

It amazed her that he caught both of her hands on the first attempt. It also amazed her that her shoulders weren't pulled out of their sockets. The jolt had her biting down on her lower lip to keep from yelling out in pain.

Holding on to her hands tightly, the knight in tarnished armor raised her up. She could see his forearms straining. They were bulging and looked rock hard as he pulled her to him. He was still hanging upside down, but he raised her up to him until they were all but face-to-face.

He was breathing heavily.

As for her breath, it had gotten completely stuck in her lungs as she found her lips less than an inch away from his mouth.

Was that a heart palpitation? Or just adrenaline rushing through her? For simplicity's sake, she decided to go with the latter.

"You're not moving," she managed to point out. If it wasn't for the way his forearms were straining, it would seem as if they were frozen in midair.

"I'm not a contortionist," he retorted. She could feel his forearms working, could feel a tremor begin to rumble through the taut, hard muscles. "Climb up!" he urged her.

"Climb up what?" she cried in complete confusion.

Was she an airhead? Had he just gone through contortions to rescue someone who was just as likely to harm his grandmother as help her?

"Me," he snapped, "damn it. Climb up me."

She hadn't the slightest idea how to do that from this position. "You're kidding."

"If I were given to kidding," he told her tersely, "which I'm not, this wouldn't be the time for me to do it. Now, get moving," he ordered sharply, "or we're both going to fall into the elevator and one of us is going to land headfirst."

That would be him. Not exactly the best way for this to end. Oh God. She could feel herself weakening.

Not now, Nika. Not now.

"Right."

Taking a breath, she released his hand and immediately grabbed hold of his torso, holding on tight.

One hand free, Cole reinforced his hold on her other hand, using both of his.

"Keep going!" he shouted at her.

She was just trying to catch her breath. "Give me a minute," she snapped at him. Her heart *really* pounded now.

He felt his grasp slipping on her. "We don't have a minute."

"Oh God."

Her heart hammering in her chest, Nika scrambled up her rescuer's body, acutely aware of its hardness and all the contours she brushed against—both his and hers— in her effort to get out of this dark, confining space.

And then she was out. Out of the car and on top of it, where the cables, the grease and an entire array of uncountable dead insects all came together. Nika huddled on top of the car, pulling her body as far into herself as she could.

Just above her head were the parted elevator doors— and light!

"Move over," Cole shouted up to her. "I want to come up."

"Sorry," she apologized. Still crouching, she tried to make herself even smaller as, attempting to move as little as possible, she shifted away from the opening. To keep from being overwhelmed by this whole ordeal, Nika forced herself not to look down. "Now what?" she asked.

He took a moment to draw in a few breaths. His hand just above her huddled body, her scowling rescuer held on to the cable. He gave her the impression that he could just swing himself off his perch like some modern-day Tarzan whenever the whim hit him.

"Isn't it obvious?" he asked her.

"It would be," she allowed magnanimously. "If my brain worked."

Fingers lightly encircling the cable, her rescuer rose to his feet, as sure-footed as if he'd been born mid-leap between skyscrapers. How could he do that? she marveled. How could he seem so casual, standing on top of the elevator car? Had he grown up on the side of a mountain?

"Now I get you up to the fourth floor," he answered glibly.

When she didn't rise on her own to stand beside him, Cole took her hand and began to tug her up to her feet. When he felt her resistance, he looked down at her expectantly.

"Look, you've got to stand up," he told her gruffly. "I can't just hurl you out the door like you were some kind of discus."

"Right." Nika exhaled, rising shakily to her feet. Her hand was tightly wrapped around his as if he was her lifeline.

It suddenly occurred to him that there might be more at play here than he'd thought. "Are you afraid of heights?"

"I wasn't when I first got on," Nika answered honestly. "But now I'm not so sure."

She was still holding on to his hand as he shifted her around so that they were both facing the parted doors on the next floor. Before she could ask him what he was doing, he'd released her hand and placed both of his on either side of her waist.

"Look up," he instructed. When she did, he said, "There's your way out."

All she could think was, *So near and yet so far.* Short

of him hurling her like that discus he'd mentioned, she couldn't see how she was going to get out. "Yes, if I was a foot taller."

His hands tightened around her waist. Something swirled around in her stomach in response. Panic?

"Don't worry, you will be," he promised. "Okay, on the count of three."

"*What* on the count of three?" She had an uneasy feeling she wasn't going to like this.

"You jump. I thrust and push."

"You what?" she demanded, twisting around so that she could look at him. He couldn't be saying what she thought he was saying.

But apparently he was already counting, albeit quietly, and "three" was on the tip of his tongue. It emerged half a split second later as he shoved her upward with a mighty thrust.

Stunned and caught off guard, Nika hadn't jumped to give her body the momentum it needed. But the man who had come to her rescue still managed to get her up to the point that she could get her arms and the upper part of her torso out between the parted doors.

Leaning her whole body into it and snaking forward, she managed to keep from sliding back down. She'd gained a hold. Not stopping to celebrate the feat, she pushed and, using her elbows in a back and forth momentum, she scrambled out a little farther.

That was when a passing orderly she was marginally familiar with saw her. Gerald Mayfield came running over to offer his help. Taking both her hands as gently as possible, he succeeded in getting her up to her feet.

The next moment, the man who'd gotten her out in

the first place was using his arms to vault himself off the roof of the same elevator car.

She swung around to look at him. There was a half-amused smile on his lips.

"Was it good for you?" he asked. "It was good for me."

"Getting out was wonderful for me," she answered, focusing only on the literal interpretation of his question. Nika stopped to take a deep breath before saying anything else. "Who *are* you?" she asked again, repeating what she'd asked him when he'd burst upside down into the elevator car.

"Are you all right, Doctor Pulaski?" Gerald asked, concerned. He seemed oblivious to the fact that he was interrupting her.

"Yes, thank you, I am." Nika started to brush herself off with the flat of her hand, resigned to the fact that it was futile. "And thanks to you," she added, turning to look at the man who had gone out of his way to extricate her from the elevator.

"Before you think I'm just some random do-gooder," he told her, brushing aside her thanks, "I want you to know that I had an ulterior motive for getting you out of there."

He caught her completely by surprise with that one. Just what kind of an ulterior motive was he talking about? She did her best to seem both game and ever-so-slightly on her guard.

He saw a ray of uncertain suspicion enter her eyes. Good. He didn't think much of people who were too naive to be suspicious. Better safe than sorry.

"You were on your way to see Ericka Baker when the elevator died on you, right?"

She eyed him quizzically. "How would you know something like that?"

Was this a new doctor on the staff whom she hadn't met yet? At this point, she had a nodding acquaintance with most of the physicians at Patience Memorial, but a few might have slipped her attention. Although, looking at this one—especially right side up—she couldn't see how that was possible.

"Did the chief of staff send you to the Geriatric Unit?" she asked.

God knew she could use the help, and it wasn't because she didn't know what she was doing. She'd worked summers while attending both undergraduate school and medical school and each position she took involved working with seniors, both veterans and private citizens, in various different hospitals. She had a very soft spot in her heart for the elderly, but there were only so many bedsides she could be at during the course of a single day. Nika was completely overwhelmed by the amount of work there was, and right now there were only two physicians in the unit to shoulder that work.

"No." Busy trying to remove several grease spots from his slacks with his handkerchief, Cole raised his head in time to see the look of disappointment on her face. "Ericka Baker's my grandmother."

Giving his slacks one more pass with the handkerchief, he frowned, gave up and shoved the oil-smudged item back into his pocket again.

"Oh." She focused on the bright side. He might not be here to help her with the patient load, but he'd come to her aid nonetheless. "I guess it's lucky for me that you're so interested in her welfare."

He nodded his head, dismissing what sounded like the beginning of a thank-you speech.

"So—" He gave her a quick once-over. "Do you need some time to pull yourself together?"

Except for a few smudges here and there, she certainly didn't look as if she needed to pull herself together, he thought. But he'd learned a long time ago that he couldn't go by appearances when it came to women. They had their own set of unique rules.

She slipped on the lab coat that she'd tied around her waist earlier, hoping she looked presentable. "No, I'm fine," she assured him. "As long as your grandmother doesn't scare easily."

To his recollection, he'd never even seen his grandmother worried, much less scared. "She has nerves of steel."

Nika laughed shortly. He found the sound had a nice, soothing ring to it.

"That puts your grandmother one up on me," Nika told him. She glanced down at her hands. There were streaks across the top of each of them. "I just need to wash my hands and I'll be ready to go." The orderly retreated back to what he was doing when he'd stopped to help, and Nika paused for a moment as she got a good look at her rescuer's slacks. She felt instantly guilty. "Oh, your pants."

Cole looked down at them himself, checking to see if they had somehow gotten worse in the last minute. Sadly, the grease stains on each leg were just as vivid.

"Guess the crease isn't as sharp as it could be," he cracked.

"I was looking at the grease," Nika said before she

realized he was being sarcastic. Getting them cleaned was her responsibility, she thought. "Give them to me."

"My pants?" he questioned, looking at her in surprise. Just what kind of a doctor was going to be treating his grandmother?

"Oh, I don't mean now," she explained quickly. Not quickly enough, she gathered, judging by his expression. "I mean, the next time you come back here to see your grandmother. I'll send them to the cleaners—or *you* can send them to the cleaners and just give me the bill."

He waved away her words. He could pay for his own dry cleaning. Or just toss the slacks away if it came down to that. The only thing this woman owed him was taking care of his grandmother.

"That's all right."

"No, it's not," she insisted firmly. He stopped walking for a moment and looked at her. She couldn't tell if he was impressed or annoyed. Either way, she pressed on. "You wouldn't have gotten that way if you hadn't come to my rescue. I believe in paying my debts, Mr. Baker."

"That's detective," he corrected her.

She's resumed walking and now it was her turn to stop first. "Mr. Detective?" she questioned, her brow furrowing.

"Detective Baker." Who the hell called anyone "Mr." Detective? He scrutinized her closely. Had she hit her head when the elevator had initially come to a stop? "You sure you're all right?"

"Yes, I'm sure." She was slightly embarrassed. "I'm just a little out of sync, that's all. It's not every day I get to climb up a man's torso to get out of an elevator car and into an elevator shaft," she told him in her own defense. "I'll be at the top of my game in a couple of minutes," she promised.

His eyes narrowed as he focused on her. "And just exactly what does this 'game' involve?" Cole asked.

She really was having trouble putting her thoughts into words this morning. Getting trapped in the elevator didn't have anything to do with it. Pulling double shifts, however, did. Someday, she would catch up on her rest and sleep for a week.

"Poor choice of words," she acknowledged. "The only 'game' in town, as far as I'm concerned, is making sure that your grandmother leaves the hospital healthier than when she came in." *I might as well make use of this man being here,* Nika thought as they turned a corner down the corridor. "Can you tell me briefly what her complaints are?"

She peered at his face as she asked the question and was rewarded to see the corners of his mouth curve ever so slightly.

The word "complaint" triggered memories of the last conversation he'd had with his grandmother before he discovered her neglected medication. "You mean other than the fact that they brought Becky Warren back from the dead?"

Nika stopped abruptly just shy of Ericka Baker's single care unit and stared at him. "Excuse me?"

"Becky Warren," he repeated. "The town 'harlot,' to quote my grandmother." And then he filled her in on the joke. "My grandmother watches *Living the Good Life* faithfully," he said, naming his grandmother's favorite soap opera. "Has for the last fifteen years. It's her only weakness—or vice. That and dark chocolate with coconut," he added. "Otherwise, she's a trouper who doesn't complain. I wouldn't have known about her heart condition if I hadn't been there for one of her 'episodes.'" He vividly remembered fearing the worst as he saw his grandmother clutch her chest, the side of her neck throbbing wildly. "Scared the hell out of me," he said as he pushed open the door to his grandmother's room. "I got her to go see Dr. Goodfellow."

Nika nodded as she walked into Ericka's room. "Good choice. He's one of the top cardiologists in the state," she informed him.

At the sound of their voices, the woman in the hospital bed turned her head toward them. The look on her finely lined face was affectionate disapproval as sharp, sapphire-blue eyes swept over the dirt and grease on Cole's clothes.

She shook her head. "Have you been making mud pies again, Coleman?" she asked.

Chapter 3

The question his grandmother asked hung in the air, unanswered.

It scraped against Cole's heart.

G wasn't teasing him the way she occasionally did, and she wasn't being witty. She was serious. He'd seen that look enter her eyes several times before. The look that silently announced that she had temporarily slipped away from him and was now off into the past. A past when she had been all things to him, including both mother and father.

Cole slanted a glance at the physician at his side, wondering if anything in his grandmother's behavior had tipped her off that the woman wasn't quite lucid.

But since this doctor he'd brought to his grandmother's bedside didn't know G, from all appearances, she seemed to be taking the remark at face value as a sign of affection between his grandmother and him.

Good.

Walking over to the older woman's bedside, Cole leaned over and kissed the weathered yet incredibly soft cheek.

"Not this time, G," he said quietly in response to her question. When he took a step back, he saw that she'd returned to her old self and he breathed a silent sigh of relief.

"Coleman, how did you manage to get so dirty?" Ericka wanted to know, clearly surprised by his less than neat appearance.

"Rescuing me," Nika told her, stepping forward.

Instead of picking up the elderly woman's chart, or accessing Ericka Baker's records on the portable computer just outside the woman's room, Nika preferred to go straight to the source and meet her patients first, then look at their records. It helped her form a relationship with the patient, however briefly it might last, and that, she'd always felt, held her in good stead. It also made the patients feel that she viewed them as people first and patients second.

But before Nika could introduce herself, the woman in the bed gave her a quick, albeit penetrating, once-over, Ericka's very blue eyes sweeping over her.

"And you are?" Ericka asked.

"Dr. Veronika Pulaski," Nika told her, putting her hand out to the woman.

She found herself on the receiving end of a handshake that was both firm and confident. No matter what the notes on the chart claimed, this was no "little old lady." This was a force to be reckoned with, Nika thought with a warm smile.

"Dr. Goodfellow asked me to run some tests on you

to make sure that the procedure he intends to perform to get your atrial fibrillation under control won't do you more harm than good."

Ericka made a small, dismissive sound, accompanying it with a wave of her hand. "He's just afraid of a lawsuit."

"No," Nika contradicted, her smile still warm as she continued focusing on the small woman, "he's afraid of putting you through something that won't result in you getting better. He is an excellent cardiovascular surgeon," she told Ericka. "Patience Memorial wouldn't give him operating privileges here if he wasn't."

"We'll see," was all Ericka was willing to concede. She shifted her eyes toward her grandson. "Coleman, you said you had some questions to ask this *very* young lady," she reminded him.

Nika picked up on the woman's inflection. "I'm not as young as I look, Mrs. Baker," she assured her.

Ericka blew out another breath. "You couldn't be," she retorted. "And don't go dismissing that particular attribute so lightly," she warned. "Someday, when you're an old lady like me, looking younger than your years will be something you'll treasure, not disclaim. Mark my words," she underscored with a look meant to pin Nika against the wall.

"You're not an old lady, G," Cole rebutted affectionately, taking her hand in both of his. "You're just a little older than I am."

"This is why I keep him around," Ericka confided to her new doctor. "He's very good for my ego. Even if he lies really badly," she added with a laugh. "Now, ask her what you want to ask her, then go before they realize they can do without you at the precinct." Her thin lips pulled into a frown as she reviewed his attire again. "And maybe you'd better stop at your place to change," Ericka added with a shake of her head. "What exactly did you rescue Dr. Pulaski from?" she asked, curious. "A garbage dump?"

When the detective didn't look as if he would answer right away, Nika was more than happy to fill his grandmother in.

"The elevator I was on got stuck between floors and the repairman wasn't going to be able to get here for a few hours." She looked across her patient's bed at the detective. "Your grandson very kindly shimmied down the elevator cables to get me out of there."

Ericka nodded, as if there was no other course her grandson could have taken. "He is a good boy," the elderly woman said proudly, giving his hand a squeeze.

Detective Cole Baker hadn't been a boy in a very long time, Nika caught herself thinking. What she first saw coming to her rescue, his legs wrapped around the cables as easily as if he was climbing down a rope in gym class, was without question *all* man.

She noted that he appeared somewhat embarrassed by his grandmother's simple declaration, even though he was trying not to show it. She decided one good rescue deserved another and came to his—verbally.

"So, what are these questions you want to ask?" Nika prompted.

He seemed surprised at her directness. Did she intend to discuss his grandmother's case in front of her? "You don't want to go somewhere private to talk?"

"Why? This is about your grandmother." Nika nodded at the woman who was listening intently to every word. "She has a right to hear whatever's said."

Ericka's thin lips spread even thinner in a pleased, wide smile.

"I like this girl, Coleman." She looked at the young woman. "Most doctors treat patients as if their minds had already evaporated. That's especially true if those patients are my age."

"I think you have every right to know and understand what's going on," Nika told her simply. She knew she would want that in the woman's place. "Dr. Goodfellow wants me to carry out a series of lab tests, and run an EEG to make sure that you're strong enough to go through this procedure. By the way, when you do have the ablation procedure," she continued as if passing the tests was a foregone conclusion, "you will have to remain awake."

Cole eyed her sharply. "They're not going to put her out?"

"No, but they will numb the area so that you won't feel any pain," she reassured both the patient and her grandson quickly. "They just want to know if something out of the ordinary happens. The best way is to keep you conscious and responsive," she told Ericka. "You'll be able to help guide them by saying if you can still feel certain things when they test different areas on your body."

This was all news to the older woman. "Well, if I'm going to help, then I shouldn't have to pay them the whole charge—" Ericka declared.

"G," Cole's tone cautioned his grandmother not to say something that could be construed argumentative.

"You won't be paying anything," Nika pointed out, opening the woman's chart. "You have Medicare and a supplementary secondary carrier. They're the ones who'll take care of the bill."

"Yes, well, it's the principle of the thing that matters," Ericka said, her voice trailing off slightly as she seemed to lose momentum.

"How long will it take?" Cole asked, turning his attention to her.

"The surgery?" Nika repeated, guessing what his question referred to. "Most ablations usually run about—"

"No, the tests," he interrupted before she could finish. "How long before you know if she can have the surgery? The last attack she had was pretty bad. It lasted over two hours."

"Tattletale," Ericka accused with an annoyed pout.

Their roles, it occurred to Cole, had somehow gotten reversed and now he was the parent and she the child. He wasn't used to this.

Nika glanced toward the woman in the bed. A hundred fifty years ago, Ericka Baker would have been viewed as the perfect prototype for a robust, determined pioneer woman. Pioneer women didn't have time to be sick. It got in their way and annoyed them.

"She doesn't like the way those palpitations have been restricting her activities." It was an educated guess on Nika's part.

He shook his head. "Not a hell of a whole lot, no. Would you?" he challenged.

"No, I wouldn't," she said honestly. "We should have everything back tomorrow, noon."

"That long?"

Gauging the duration was all in the eyes of the beholder. Nika laughed. "There was a time when a simple appendectomy kept a patient in the hospital for two weeks," she told him. "In comparison, this is pretty fast and streamlined."

She could see that her answer didn't satisfy him. Hard man to please, she thought. But he wasn't her concern. His grandmother was. "I'll call in a favor and we'll bump you up to the head of the line," she promised Ericka. "It's the least I can do, seeing as how your grandson rescued me."

Ericka nodded again, somewhat placated. "Sounds only fair," she agreed, glancing toward Cole.

Time for him to go, Nika thought, even though there was something about his presence that was oddly unsettling and yet exciting at the same time. Neither had a place within the framework of her duties.

"And now, Detective, I'm afraid I'm going to have to ask you to make yourself scarce," she told him.

Not that he planned on staying any longer—the meeting was swiftly breathing down his neck—but having this snippet of a doctor push him out of the room like this raised red flags for him.

"Why?" he asked.

"Because I'm going to have to examine your grandmother now," she told him patiently, "and I think it would be more comfortable for her if you respectfully waited just outside the door."

He looked at his grandmother and then quickly looked away. It was hard to say if he was more embarrassed for himself, or for the older woman.

"Oh, yeah, well—" Heat rose up along his neck, causing it to turn an unnatural shade of reddish-pink. He was already at the door, turning the doorknob. "I'll come by after my shift, G." He tossed the words over his shoulder, along with one last quick glance.

"Unless some pretty girl nabs you," Ericka qualified, raising her voice to be heard.

He paused, shaking his head. The woman was always trying to get him to pair up with someone. "Not likely," he told her. "See you tonight," he added quickly, stepping outside the room.

And then he turned around to see if his grandmother's doctor was behind him. She was.

"Doctor, here's my card." He thrust the small, white card with its dramatic black lettering at her. "Call me if something goes wrong." It wasn't a request but an order. "You can reach me at the last number on the bottom anytime." He tapped it with his forefinger. "Anytime, night or day," he emphasized.

Nika slipped out of the room for a moment, easing the door closed behind her. It touched her that he was so concerned. Looking at him, at his chiseled features and the hard set of his mouth, she would have said that he didn't particularly care deeply about anyone—including himself. There was nothing soft about him, nothing vulnerable to indicate intense concern on any level.

Just went to show that you definitely couldn't judge a book by its cover, she told herself. Not even after the first few pages were glimpsed.

Her hand closed over the card he'd offered her and she tucked it into her pocket.

"I won't have to use it," she assured him kindly. "Your grandmother strikes me as a woman who can more than meet any kind of curve that life has to throw at her and come out smiling."

"She used to be," he acknowledged and a strain of sadness, which he couldn't quite cover, echoed in his voice. "But that was before she got this old."

Nika had known her patient for a total of less than five minutes so far, but some things she could just instinctively sense from the very beginning.

"I wouldn't let your grandmother hear you say that if I were you," Nika advised. "Otherwise, you're going to have to be sleeping with one eye open for the rest of your life."

It wouldn't be the first time he'd had to sleep lightly, he thought, thinking back to some of the undercover cases he'd worked. But he saw no reason to say anything about that to this woman. This wasn't about him, it was about his grandmother. About keeping her well and thriving the way she always had been.

"Keep the card anyway," he told her. "Just in case. It'll make both of us feel better."

"Us?" she questioned uncertainly.

"My grandmother and me."

"Oh. Of course." What was she thinking? Why in heaven's name would the man be making a reference to the two of them as "us"? Of course he was referring to himself and his grandmother.

That stretch in the elevator addled you more than you're willing to admit, Nika, she upbraided herself. *Get a grip.*

Nika rallied, pushing on, as the detective, satisfied that he'd made himself clear, started to leave. "And don't forget to give me your bill," she called after him.

He didn't bother turning around or answering her. He just kept walking.

"Um, Nika, I don't know if anyone's explained this to you, but eventually, we're supposed to be charging them for our services, not the other way around," an amused female voice said behind her.

Turning around, Nika saw that she'd guessed right. Her older sister—older only by eleven months—stood behind her. It was amazing, though, how much Alyx sounded like Sasha, her oldest cousin and the very first Dr. Pulaski to come to this hospital.

"Alyx, what are you doing here?" Nika asked. And even as she formed the words, the answer came to her and her whole countenance lit up. "Did they send you here to help me?" She tried to recall if Alyx had mentioned anything about having the flu. She couldn't remember.

"No, I snuck up here as soon as I heard. I wanted to make sure you were okay." Alyx's eyes washed over her quickly, taking inventory of every limb.

"Heard? Heard what?"

"Someone in the E.R. told me that there was a resident stuck in an elevator in between floors," Alyx told her.

Nika looked at her, a little surprised. "And you immediately thought of me?" she questioned, then pointed out the obvious before her sister could answer. "Alyx, I'm not the only resident that this hospital has."

Alyx raised her slender shoulders. "What can I tell you? Some of Mama's paranoia rubbed off on me." She looked down at a particularly dark streak of dirt on her sister's lab coat. It was all the evidence that was needed. "It was you, wasn't it?"

"Busted." Nika laughed. She was already moving away. "But I don't have time to talk about it right now. I have a patient to get back to." *One of many,* she added silently. Nika nodded toward Ericka's door. "I'll tell you all about it tonight, I promise. Call me when you're free. *If* you're free," she qualified, thinking of the very handsome policeman her sister had introduced her to when she'd arrived. The policeman who had arrested Alyx's heart and placed it behind bars for all eternity. Alyx was going to be the first of them to get married, Nikka thought, with a little mistiness tugging at her soul.

"And you'll start by explaining what you're offering that somber-looking hunk money for?" Alyx asked, still standing where she was.

"A clean breast of everything," Nika promised, crossing her heart with her forefinger.

Not knowing the whole story immediately, she could see, was all but killing her older sister. Alyx had always been insatiable when it came to her curiosity. She always had to know everything about everything.

"It's not nearly as exciting as you think," was the only crumb she had time to toss her sister before she hurried back into Ericka Baker's room.

"About time you came back," Ericka said, her eyes narrowing as she looked at her doctor. "I thought maybe you decided to run off with my grandson."

Nika flashed a smile at the woman as she took her stethoscope out of her pocket. "Sorry to disappoint you, no running off."

"I'm not the one who's disappointed," Ericka informed her with conviction.

"Oh? And just who would be the one who's disappointed?" Nika asked, humoring the woman.

Ericka didn't answer her. Instead, the elderly woman merely watched her intently, her message silently conveyed.

And then, sitting up straighter, Ericka announced, "Let's get this show on the road already," and began to unbutton the top of her nightgown—she'd brought her own, no doubt refusing to be caught dead in the one that the hospital issued.

"Not so fast, Mrs. Baker," Nika cautioned, placing her hand over her patient's to stop the older woman from disrobing. "There's a little matter of a history and physical to get out of the way first."

Ericka seemed somewhat annoyed and very impatient. "Nothing's changed since I saw my doctor two days ago," the woman told her.

"That might be true," Nika agreed, humoring her, "but I need to acquaint myself with you and I've never taken down your history before."

Very slowly, a smile of approval slipped over the older woman's lips. "Believe in crossing your t's and dotting your i's, do you?"

"Every time," Nika told her.

"Not a bad quality, I guess." She didn't quite succeed in sounding indifferent. Ericka eyed the physician's left hand. "You married?"

She thought of her mother, who had been crusading for each of her daughters to get married since Alyx turned twenty. She was desperate to be a grandmother—and have more grandchildren than Uncle Josef and Aunt Magda. "No, I'm not."

"Planning to be?" Mrs. Baker prodded, watching her carefully as she answered.

"Someday, yes." But that someday was a long way in the future, Nika added silently. She wanted to get a practice going, wanted to do things that really mattered first. If marriage was in the cards for her, it would happen. But there was enough time to worry about that later.

Ericka cocked her head, still looking at her closely, her expression saying that she was confident she could detect a lie if she heard one. "So there's no one important in your life right now?"

"You, Mrs. Baker," Nika told her warmly as she prepared to take the woman's blood pressure. "You're important in my life."

Ericka frowned. "Is that your hokey way of telling me that you're dedicated?"

"You might say that," Nika allowed with a laugh. "It's also a 'hokey' way of saying that I care about my patients. Every one of them. And since you're one of my patients…"

Ericka nodded her head, holding up her hand to keep her doctor from continuing. "I get it. You care about me. Well, if you do, it's nice to know. Now," the old woman instructed as she braced herself and raised her chin, "do your worst."

"What I plan to do, Mrs. Baker," Nika told her gently, "is my very best."

Ericka's head bobbed curtly. "I'll let you know if you succeed."

Nika pressed her lips together. She'd come to learn that patients didn't like it when you laughed at what they said, unless they were intentionally trying to be funny. "I'm counting on it," she told the woman.

Chapter 4

Nika frowned as she appraised the upper and lower numbers on the blood pressure gauge in her hand. They weren't what she wanted them to be, especially since the woman in the bed was on blood pressure medication.

"It's a little high," she told Ericka as she deflated the cuff. Pausing to make a quick notation of the reading on the woman's chart, Nika swiftly unwrapped the cuff from the thin arm.

Ericka waved away the note of concern. "Of course it's high. My new doctor kept me waiting. I got aggravated."

Nika looked at her. She knew the woman knew better than that. "That wouldn't have caused your blood pressure to elevate like that unless you were waiting for me in a yard full of pit bulls." She tucked the cuff away. "I'd like to see that come down a little bit before we finally whisk you off for surgery."

Ericka made a noise that sounded very much like a snort. "You forfeited the 'whisking' part by making me take all these tests you're talking about first."

Nika placed a placating hand on top of one of the woman's blue-veined hands and said gently, "Mrs. Baker, the object here is to make you well, not to see how fast we can get you in and out of the hospital. We don't take chances with our patients' lives here."

Ericka looked at her for a long moment, as if assessing the genuineness of the statement. And then her sharper features melted into a softer expression as she smiled.

"Call me G," she urged.

Nika cocked her head. She'd heard the detective refer to the woman that way. Was it her middle initial, or the first letter of some kind of nickname?

"G?" Nika repeated, an unspoken question in her voice.

The platinum-blond head nodded. "That's what I told Coleman to call me when he first came to live with me. I hated the way Grandmother sounded. Still do. Makes me think of some old, bent-over woman, shuffling around in sensible shoes, her white hair pulled back in a bun at the nape of her neck." Finished with her description, Ericka shivered.

"No worries," Nika told her with a laugh. "That certainly doesn't begin to describe you. I thought the computer made a mistake when I looked down at your chart earlier. If ever a woman didn't look anywhere close to eighty-four, it's you."

Ericka positively beamed. "You know, you just might have become my new best friend after all," the older woman told her.

"I'll settle for being the doctor who makes you feel well enough to go home, Mrs.— G." About to use the woman's last name, Nika corrected herself at the last moment.

"Fair enough," Ericka declared. "Continue," she urged, indicating that she was ready to endure the rest of the physical.

Nika suppressed her smile and did as she was "bidden."

She had just finished the feisty woman's exam and was carefully entering the last of her notes on the chart when the sound jolted her. Piercing the late morning air, the alarm sounded a great deal like an air raid siren used in one of those old movies depicting Europe during World War II.

Except that this wasn't an air raid. And rather than warning of a possible multitude of deaths, this had to do with only one possible demise. But even one was one too many.

She didn't want to have another on the books if she could help it.

Nika instantly abandoned the chart, setting it down on a side counter.

"What is that awful noise?" Ericka asked as she put her hands over her ears and tried to press out the sound.

"I'll put down you have good hearing when I get back," Nika promised, trying to divert the woman's curiosity from the reason that the alarm was going off. She didn't want the woman frightened—and she definitely didn't want her to start wondering if perhaps that alarm would ever go off for her.

"What's going on?" Ericka demanded, shouting in order to be heard.

"It's a code blue," was all Nika said before she ran out into the hall—making sure she closed the door to Ericka's room behind her.

The sound that signaled the very real possibility of someone's life ebbing away filled the hallway, making it momentarily impossible for her to ascertain from which direction the alarm was coming. The next moment, Nika had her answer. Alerted by the monitor at the nurses' station, the two responding nurses and an orderly were all running toward one room.

A quick scrutiny told Nika that so far, no doctor was coming to the patient's aid. They were still incredibly shorthanded.

"Crash cart," she yelled out to the other three. "We're going to need a crash cart."

The orderly, Gerald Mayfield, a powerful-looking man who was almost as wide as he was tall and had helped get her out of the elevator earlier, fell back to fetch the lifesaving device.

She knew who the room belonged to a second before she entered. John Kelly. She'd paused to talk to the man this morning just before she'd gone down to the cafeteria. And subsequently gotten stuck in the elevator on her way back, she thought ruefully. Maybe if she'd taken the stairs, she would have gotten back sooner and somehow could have prevented this.

God knew how, she thought now, looking at the painfully thin man whose heart had abruptly stopped beating.

The monitor attached to him, tracking his vital signs, had nothing to show for its efforts but very thin, straight lines. They were accompanied by an eerie, flat note that mournfully announced the end of a life.

"There's no pulse, Doctor," Katie O'Connor, one of the two nurses who'd made it to the patient's room first, told her. The nurse's long fingers were still pressed against the elderly man's throat, as if that would somehow make his vital signs magically reappear once again.

But they didn't. The straight lines on the monitor continued going nowhere.

It couldn't end this quickly, Nika silently argued in her head.

"He was just talking to me," she said out loud, addressing her words to Katie. "Telling me how much he was looking forward to going back to the nursing home because he'd figured out a chess move that would confound his roommate. He was positively gleeful about it. He didn't sound or behave like a man who was about to die," she added, saying the words more to herself than to the other two women.

Katie, who'd been a nurse more years than she'd willingly admit, looked at her with sympathy. "Can't always tell by the way they look, Doctor."

She knew that. And yet…

Behind her, Gerald was coming in, pushing the crash cart before him.

"Charge 'em," Nika ordered, grabbing the defibrillator paddles. She held them up while Gerald quickly covered both surfaces with a gel. Rubbing them together, Nika called out, "Clear!" before applying both paddles to Kelly's chest.

His body convulsed in response, clearing the mattress in some places, but ultimately the former police sergeant didn't awaken from what appeared to be his now permanent sleep.

Nika didn't want to let him go.

"C'mon, Mr. Kelly, you've got a chess game to finish, remember? You wanted to show Don that he couldn't just come in and be the center of attention, remember? Don't wimp out on me now," she pleaded. Glancing over her shoulder, she looked at the nurse who was now at the controls of the defibrillator. "Again!" The next moment, with the amps raised, Nika cried "Clear!" and tried to revive the man again.

With the same results.

Twice more she made the retired police sergeant's body go through its macabre, lifeless dance and had the exact same results each time.

Holding the paddles, she saw the two nurses and the orderly looking at her, waiting. Silently telling her to do what she knew she had to do.

Call it.

She released the sigh that was rattling around in her chest. "Time of death—eleven twenty-three," Nika pronounced quietly and then returned the paddles to the cart.

"You did everything you could do, Doctor," Katie told her sympathetically. "It was just his time to go," the grandmother of five added softly.

"Besides," the other nurse, Jenna, chimed in, "where he's going is a lot better than where he would have gone if you'd brought him back from the brink," she assured Nika with the confidence of the very young who never doubted themselves. "Have you *seen* that nursing home he was living in?" Jenna, all of twentysomething, shivered to make her point. "If that's the way I'm going to end up, shoot me now."

"Hey, a little respect for the dead," Gerald chided sharply. Jenna frowned and fell into a brooding silence as she slowly stripped the deceased man of the various tubes and wires that had been connected to him. Gerald spared Nika a compassionate look. "Death's all part of it, Dr. Pulaski," he told her philosophically. "You shouldn't take it so hard."

The orderly was right. After all, what did she expect, Nika asked herself. She was working in the Geriatrics Unit, for heaven's sake. These were *old* people. A lot of them had overtaxed their immune systems and were susceptible to so many different things, things that could fell them without a moment's notice.

That was why they were running understaffed in this unit, because of the threat of someone unwittingly bringing in the flu. They couldn't control the visitors who came in—although, sadly, a lot of these patients *had* no one to visit them—but they could at least control the staff's interactions with the patients.

Nika nodded in response to what the orderly said. She forced herself to focus on the steps she had to take next, not on what had just happened.

"I guess it just seems like a lot of these old people have been dying lately," she murmured. And death was not something she would *ever* get used to.

"That's because they have," Katie told her. She went about tidying the man up so that he had a little dignity left, even in death. "They're old people," she emphasized, just as Nika had in her mind. "It goes with the territory and is to be expected. It's a lot harder to handle when you lose a patient in the pediatrics ward," she pointed out. "At least these people have had relatively full lives."

Nika nodded, then squared her shoulders, silently telling herself to get over it, to straighten up and fly right. She'd do none of her remaining patients any good if she allowed herself to break down and cry.

"You're right," she told Katie.

The woman grinned broadly. "Of course I'm right. It's in my contract," Katie told her with a wink. "Go help your living patients. There's nothing more you can do for Mr. Kelly. We'll do what needs to be done for him now," the nurse assured her, taking charge.

"I should notify the next of kin," Nika said, more to herself than to Katie. The very idea filled her with a sense of dread. This was the ultimate in bad news, no matter how prepared a loved one might think that they were.

"There isn't any," Jenna told her, practically chirping out the information. "Nobody to notify. Except for maybe the nursing home," she added as an afterthought. "They'll want to know so that they can get his room ready for someone else."

That sounded so cold. So detached. *Business as usual, nothing more.* Damn, she hated this part of her world.

Out loud, Nika said nothing. She looked at the two nurses and the orderly. They were all doing their part, unfazed, preparing the old man for his last exit. Would she ever get to that state? Would she get to the point where death rolled right off her back, and it didn't feel as if the specter had taken a large chunk out of her heart when she lost a patient?

As if reading her mind, Katie leaned in as she moved past her. "You let it get to you, you're no help to the rest of them—the ones who still need you to make a difference in their lives. Remember that."

Nika nodded and whispered, "Thank you," before she left the room.

It took her a few minutes to get the tears under control.

"You look terrible," Sasha declared, almost walking into her cousin. She was on her way in and Nika appeared to be on her way out. "Who died?" she asked.

Nika paused and followed her cousin back inside for a second. "Mr. Kelly," she told Sasha quietly.

Sasha's eyes widened with surprise—and distress. "Oh God, Nika, I'm sorry. It was just an expression. I didn't realize someone had actually died," she apologized, chagrined. "Was he a patient of yours?"

"Right now, they're all patients of mine on that floor. The Geriatrics Unit," she said in case Sasha wasn't aware of where her rotation had taken her. Something had been gnawing at her since she'd put it into words earlier. "Since I've come to work in the unit, it feels like a lot more people have died."

There was nothing but sympathy on Sasha's face. "And that means you're what, the angel of death? Things happen, honey. Old people do die. What do you mean by 'more,' exactly?"

"More than the average expected number," Nika answered. She saw the skeptical look on her cousin's face. "I minored in math," she explained.

"Good to know. Next time I'm in a jam, I'll bring my checkbook to you. I can't count higher than ten without taking off my shoes." She slipped a comforting arm around her cousin's shoulders despite the fact that Nika was several inches taller than she was. "Honey, again, they're old people. They're in the hospital, which means they're sick. A lot of them are worn out. The odds are against them and those odds get worse every day." She saw that Nika wasn't completely at ease. "Look, if you're really worried that something isn't quite right, why don't you run this past Dad? Or Tony?" Sasha suggested, referring to her husband, who was a detective in the homicide division of the NYPD. She reached into her pocket to take out her cell. "I could call Tony for you—"

Nika put her hand over her cousin's phone. Gently, she pushed it back into the pocket it had come from. "That's okay, maybe I'm just being overly sensitive."

"FYI, patients think that's a good quality in a doctor," Sasha told her. She was about to say something more, but her pager went off. She angled the device that was clipped onto her belt. "After five false alarms, it looks like Mrs. Davis's water finally broke. Thank God!" she declared happily. "Gotta run, Nika." And yet, she still paused long enough to give her cousin's face another once-over. "You'll be all right?" she asked, concerned.

"I'll be fine." She waved Sasha on. "Go, do what you do best. Bring another little taxpayer into the world," she urged with a smile.

The moment her cousin was out of sight, the smile on Nika's face vanished, replaced by a weary expression. She wasn't being overly sensitive. That was just an excuse she'd given Sasha. And she also didn't believe that the way she was feeling was the product of an overactive imagination. Older patients on her floor *were* expiring at a rate that she was definitely uncomfortable about.

Okay, it wasn't in droves, but still…

Granted, there had been more admissions to the unit of late than there used to be. She'd checked into that via a comparison between last year's admissions at this time and now. More people meant that the number of patients dying increased. But so had the percentages and that part was odd.

She's lost five patients in two months. Okay, so three of them were diagnosed with terminal diseases and death was an almost merciful release—but getting cured would have been even better.

Was it just a coincidence, or was there something else going on? Something that she was missing?

She hadn't a clue, but her gut warned her of some kind of pattern. Still, she didn't want to mention her suspicion to her family. She didn't know them all that well yet and the last thing she wanted was for them to think that she was the kind of person who went around seeing ghosts when there weren't any or stirring up trouble as she went along. She wasn't a rabble-rouser, just a concerned doctor.

What she needed was an impartial outsider who, by the way, was also acquainted with police procedure and could figure out if something not quite aboveboard was going on.

Frustrated, she shoved her hands into her pockets, pensively reviewing her options. Her fingers came in contact with card stock.

Nika realized what it was before she had a chance to pull it out all the way and look at it.

Cole Baker's business card.

Detective Cole Baker's business card, she amended, her mind going from zero to sixty-five in just under a racing heartbeat. She had no idea if he'd be open to looking into this for her, but there was nothing to be lost by asking him. He couldn't hold that against her, she reasoned as his frowning, disapproving face rose up in her mind's eye. She was just being a concerned citizen, that was all.

She lost no time in dialing his cell phone number.

The line went active on the second ring. The detective surprised her with his prompt response. She could hear street noise in the background. They all but drowned him out.

"This is Baker."

Did he ever sound anything but impatient, she wondered. "Detective Baker, this is Dr. Pulaski calling—"

Impatience turned to gruffness instantly. "What's happened to my grandmother?" he demanded.

A voice in her head told her her meddling was an all-round bad idea. If she had concerns, there were proper channels to go through. She could—and should—go to the hospital administrator and talk to Ella about what was on her mind. She owed the woman that, rather than going over her head and calling in the police. What if she was completely off the mark? She didn't want to embarrass the hospital, and that would be exactly what she'd be doing—not to mention committing medical suicide with her career.

"Nothing happened to your grandmother," she assured him.

"Then why are you calling?" he asked. It was obvious he didn't believe her.

The level of background noise increased, making it hard for her to hear. But she pressed on. She had to give him some kind of reason for calling, otherwise he would think that his grandmother's fate was in the hands of a lunatic. "Do you have any idea if she's always had high blood pressure?"

"I didn't know it was high at all," he confessed. Damn it, why hadn't his grandmother told him? Why were all the surprises attached to her case bad? "Why, is that a problem?"

"It might be," she acknowledged, treading cautiously. She didn't want to alarm him. "I'll confess that I'd like to see it significantly lower before we go ahead with the procedure."

"What about her other tests?" he asked. "What do they say?"

She'd forgotten about them. "Nothing yet. We haven't gotten back any of the results. They should be in first thing in the morning," she promised him, then, because she had a feeling he was expecting it, she added, "I'll be in touch with you the minute they turn up. Thanks for the information," she told him and then, with that, she terminated the call.

With a deep sigh, she put her cell phone back on vibrate and pocketed it. She debated the wisdom of her next move for approximately two minutes, decided that she couldn't live with herself if she said nothing and her instincts ultimately turned out to be right—that something more than natural progression caused these people to die.

Squaring her shoulders, she forgot about taking a late lunch and went to talk to the person she should have discussed this with in the first place, the hospital administrator.

While her office was being renovated, the administrator had temporarily relocated to the second floor. Nika took the stairs.

Chapter 5

"And your contention is what exactly?" Ella Silverman asked, looking at Nika over the top of her reading glasses. They had slipped down again and the woman had left them there, temporarily suspending the ongoing battle with gravity that required her to push them up the bridge of her nose every few minutes.

As quickly and succinctly as she could, Nika had told the tall, imposing, frowning hospital administrator that she was uneasy about the number of recent deaths in the Geriatrics Unit. The moment the words had left her mouth, she could have sworn that Ella Silverman had instantly looked like someone who'd gone on the defensive.

Nika chose her words carefully as she repeated her concern.

"Just that the patients in the Geratrics Unit are dying at almost twice the national average for their age group."

The woman's back literally went up. Ella narrowed her eyes. "And you know this how?"

Nika wasn't about to back off now. "Research."

"I see." Ella tossed her head. Since her shoe-polish-black hair was frozen in place with a third of a can of hair spray, not a single hair moved out of place. Despite the administrator's caricaturelike appearance, Nika knew through word of mouth that the woman was actually very good at her job, but she was a bit overly chauvinistic when it came to protecting the hospital's reputation.

"Are you insinuating that the patients are dying because the quality of the care they are receiving here is poor? Or are you saying that the hospital is in some way failing to provide as clean and germfree an environment for these patients as possible?" She held up her hand before Nika could begin to answer, warning her. "And before you answer, I would think very carefully about the next words I say if I were you."

"No, no," Nika denied the two suggestions Ella had offered with enthusiasm. "I'm not saying it's either of those reasons."

Ella sighed, exasperation echoing in the sound. "So exactly what is it that you *are* saying, Dr. Pulaski? That the hospital is having some kind of run of bad luck, having these people come here to be treated in our Geriatrics Unit only to die?" the woman asked sharply. She pretended to frame a public service announcement. "'People, keep your parents and beloved Uncle Oscar out of Patience Memorial if you don't want them to die on you.' Is *that* what you're implying, Dr. Pulaski?" she asked, leaning over her desk and somehow managing to fill the space around Nika with her presence.

Maybe she should have gone to her uncle after all, Nika thought. At least Uncle Josef listened and let her finish when she spoke. He didn't immediately go on the defensive the way Ms. Silverman was obviously doing.

"No, ma'am, I'm not implying that the hospital is at fault in any way." And she really wasn't. She supposed that her intention in coming here was to use the hospital administrator as a sounding board. She'd had better ideas, she now thought ruefully.

"Then what *are* you saying?" the woman demanded irritably.

Nika tried to salvage the situation by falling back on a technical question. "Have any of these last few deaths been looked into?" She could see by the woman's expression that she wasn't making herself clear. "Have any of them had an autopsy performed?"

"An autopsy?" Ella cried. "No. None of their deaths were suspicious," she retorted, enunciating each word slowly and carefully as if in doing so, she'd crush the argument. "There was no reason for an autopsy," she said with finality, "not to mention that there's no money to conduct one on a whim."

Nika pressed her lips together. "This last patient who just died this morning, Mr. Kelly, they said he had no family. If no one steps forward to claim his body, maybe you could authorize—"

Ella's glare was frosty and she succeeded in freezing what Nika was about to say in midsentence. "There's no money for anything 'extra.' In case you don't know this, the hospital's budget is stretched to the very limit as it is." Like a queen who'd grown tired of the conversation, Ella straightened, indicating that the audience was over. "Now, unless you have some hard and fast evidence to present—"

"Not without an autopsy," Nika pointed out, still hoping that the hospital administrator would change her mind.

The exact opposite happened. Ella took that as a sign that the discussion was terminated. "Well, there you have it, then," she announced with a wave of her hand. "The subject is closed, Doctor. Now, if you'll excuse me, I have work to do. *Real* work," she underscored, looking back at the report she'd been reading before Nika had asked to speak with her.

"Sorry to have bothered you," Nika muttered, withdrawing.

"No bother," the woman replied without looking up. "My door is always open," she added, repeating her very worn public mantra.

In contrast to your mind, Nika thought as she left the room.

Well, she'd tried, she told herself. And maybe Ms. Silverman was ultimately right. Maybe there was nothing more to it than a perverse kind of misfortune, an anomaly that just happened to have shown up at this hospital instead of another one.

Why didn't that make her feel any better about the situation?

Nika went away troubled, vowing to pay more close attention to as many details as she could. And most likely to give up sleep for the next few months, she thought wearily.

"How is she doing?"

The voice, deep and resonant, seemed to come out of

nowhere. And succeeded in scaring the hell out of her because Nika was so caught up in what she was reading in one of the reports she'd managed to get off the computer at the nurses' station. The report was a history and physical of one of the deceased patients. An elderly woman with leukemia. A condition that had mysteriously and miraculously gone into remission. Just before she died.

Stifling a scream, Nika swung around to look behind her.

"Hey, sorry. Didn't mean to scare you like that," Cole apologized.

On his way to see his grandmother, he'd spotted the young doctor standing off to the side, reading. He'd decided to stop and ask about the tests that had been taken earlier today. He figured it was too soon for answers, but the way technology was moving forward these days, he took a shot at it. He hadn't expected Nika Pulaski to almost jump out of her skin.

"Is everything all right?" he asked. "You seem a little jumpy."

It was unclear to Nika if the tall, dark and brooding police detective was asking after her well-being, or if his question ultimately worked its way back to his grandmother's condition.

She decided that he had to be wondering about the old woman, so she focused on that, even as she told herself she would have to get her nerves under control.

Nika pressed the papers she had against her chest so that he couldn't see the name that was on top. It never hurt to be cautious, even it if wasn't ordinarily in her nature, she told herself.

"Your grandmother hasn't had any episodes since

you left, if that's what you're referring to. And if all the tests come back with the right readings, then we're a go for surgery tomorrow afternoon at four."

"Four," Cole repeated skeptically. Seemed like a bad time of day to him. He would have wanted the surgeon to operate on his grandmother first thing in the morning. "Won't the doctor be tired by then? Less sharp?"

"Dr. Goodfellow won't operate if he feels something might impede the best possible outcome for the patient. And that works both ways."

"Both ways?" he questioned. What was she talking about?

Nika nodded. "I was told that he once stopped a surgery two minutes before it was about to begin because the patient had changed his mind and didn't want the procedure done. Goodfellow didn't try to talk him into it, or just chalk it up to the patient having cold feet. He stopped everything dead. Your grandmother is in very good hands," she assured the detective.

"Maybe," he allowed and then he asked, "Will you be assisting?"

Nika smiled proudly. The doctor had asked her to assist just this morning. "As a matter of fact, yes. Mostly, I'll just be standing there and observing," she confessed, knowing how these things went, "but if you'd like to request someone with more years of experience, I could let the woman who schedules Dr. Goodfellow's surgeries know and—"

"That won't be necessary," Cole said, cutting her short. He had a feeling that the doctor could go on talking indefinitely if she was unchecked. "I think you're qualified enough to stand and watch," he told her. "As long as they don't give you anything sharp to work with while you're being jumpy." It was meant as a joke, but he saw that the mild attempt at humor didn't seem to register with her. He looked at her more closely. There was a somberness in her eyes he didn't know what to make of. "You sure nothing's wrong?" he asked.

Nika wasn't sure what made her confess. Ordinarily, she kept her own counsel when there was no one she felt comfortable talking to. But her brief, unfruitful meeting with Ms. Silverman had left a really bad taste in her mouth and, before she was actually aware of what she was doing, she found herself sharing what had sent her to the hospital administrator's office in the first place.

"One of my patients died today."

He immediately related the occurrence to his grandmother being there.

"Because of a surgery?" he asked. Was she trying to subtly tell him something, or was he just worrying because life and his job had made him paranoid?

"No. Mr. Kelly died in his room in the Geriatrics Unit. I'm not sure why. I was just talking to him this morning. His discharge papers were being prepared and he was set to be transported back to the nursing home later today." She blew out a deep breath, thinking how ironic life could be. Here one moment, gone in the next blink of an eye. "Instead, he's in the morgue now, waiting to be claimed by someone or wind up being buried in the city's version of a potter's field." The man had seemed so vital, so eager to get back and beat his friend at chess. "I can't believe he died just like that."

"What did he die of?" Cole asked.

"Unofficially?" Nika nodded. "His heart stopped." That was what was being written down on the death certificate.

"That'll do it every time," Cole commented. From all indications, this doctor had nothing new to share with him. That meant he should be on his way to go see his grandmother. Instead, he lingered a moment or two longer and shared an observation he'd made.

"That wasn't just lip service you were giving me earlier, was it?" He watched her eyebrows draw together in a silent query. "You really do care about these patients."

Well, at this stage of the game, she certainly wasn't in it for the money. For the pleasure of pulling double shifts and turning into almost a zombie, as a resident she was getting somewhere in the neighborhood of forty thousand dollars a year. To be honest, she wasn't altogether sure just what the exact sum was. But that didn't matter because that wasn't why she was doing it.

"Of course I care," she told him with feeling. "I wouldn't be in this if I didn't care—although Mama had other ideas," she recalled with a touch of fondness. She knew—or believed she knew—all of her mother's flaws and she still loved the woman, still accepted, for the most part, the way her mother was.

In the long run, though they'd had their clashes, she was grateful to her mother. It couldn't have been easy, raising four daughters all alone, even if she did have Aunt Zofia around for moral support.

"Mama?" he questioned. Who called their mother Mama these days? He assumed she was referring to a grandmother. His own hadn't liked the title, which is how he'd come up with calling her G.

"My mother," Nika answered, not seeing where the mystery was.

Okay, so maybe this doctor was the old-fashioned type. It was rare, but there was nothing wrong with that, he thought. In a way, he kind of found it intriguing. "Your mother wanted you to be a doctor?"

Wanted was a very weak word in this case. *Demanded* was more like it, but she let that go. What she did say was, "She wanted *all* of us to be doctors."

"All of you," he repeated, waiting.

The silent question was obvious, Nika thought. The detective wanted the term *all* defined.

"My sisters and me. There're four of us," she added before he could raise a quizzical brow again.

Four. Four doctors, no less. He had to admit that was impressive. Cole thought of what the average higher education cost these days, and just how much he'd had to scrape together in order to earn an undergraduate degree in criminology.

"Your mother certainly had lofty ambitions for you and your sisters."

It wasn't exactly as noble as it might sound, she thought. "Actually, I'd say she was probably more driven by a sense of competition than ambition."

He was silent for a moment as he tried to make sense out of what she'd just said, then shook his head. "I don't think I understand," he told her. "As a matter of fact, I *know* I don't understand."

"It's very simple, really. My aunt and uncle have five daughters. They all became doctors. After my father died, my mother carried around a lot of resentment toward my uncle and, well…" Her voice trailed off for a moment and then she shrugged. "Well, you get the picture."

It wasn't hard to fill in the blanks. Most families were far from ideal. His own mother was a perfect example of that. "Yeah, I do. Sometimes parents don't always think clearly."

As he said it, Nika had the impression that Cole wasn't talking about her mother any longer. Curious, she forced herself to table the questions that immediately arose in her mind. Something about the detective reminded her of a knight in tarnished armor and warned her not to ask too many questions—unless she wanted to get rebuffed. She had the feeling that Cole Baker wasn't the type who shared his thoughts, his feelings, or his past easily with others.

She could feel him withdrawing even as he still remained standing there. His next words bore out her impression.

"Well, I'd better go see my grandmother before she puts out an APB—an all points bulletin," Cole elaborated.

"I know what APB means," she told him with a smile, then added, "I get to watch crime dramas on TV sometimes." He started to turn away. "Before you go," she interjected.

Stopping, Cole looked at her over his shoulder. "Yes?"

"There's something else." The moment she said the sentence, she saw his face become rigid. He was on his guard again.

Any tiny headway she might have made with the man instantly vanished. He was a man who didn't trust easily, she thought. A man who always expected the worst. What had happened in his life to make him that way? she couldn't help wondering. Whatever it was had crushed him—but not completely. Because if it had, he wouldn't have rescued her, no matter what the excuse. He would have stood on the sidelines and let someone else do it, telling himself it was none of his concern.

"Yes?" he asked warily.

"I have to tell you that I'm still a little concerned about your grandmother's blood pressure. Luckily, the procedure Dr. Goodfellow is ultimately going to perform requires only a local anesthetic—"

"You already said that," he reminded her, a note of impatience breaking through. It was, she thought, as if he was waiting for some sort of bombshell to drop. But there was no bombshell. She'd told him what her concern was.

"My point is that a local isn't as hard on a person's body as a general anesthetic is," she explained. "If the surgery your grandmother was having done needed a general anesthetic, I'd advise holding off on performing it until such time as we get her blood pressure under control."

"Is her blood pressure really that bad?" he asked.

"It's not astronomical. I've heard of patients who had elevated readings double what your grandmother has and they went on to live long lives. However, blood pressure can spike both when a person is being put under and being brought out of anesthesia, and that's when a stroke can happen. Or worse. It's best to have her blood pressure within acceptable parameters just to stay on the safe side. I don't like taking any kind of chances with my patients, unless there are no other options."

Offhand, he would have said that she sounded sincere. He wondered if it was an act. There was a time when he would have bet everything he had in the world that his mother loved him—and she'd tried to kill him just before she'd turned the gun on herself.

"I'll keep that in mind. Anything else?" he asked.

Nika pressed her lips together. She found herself

fighting an urge. She really wanted to share her uneasiness about the recent deaths with someone, and who better than a near stranger—even if he was as sexy as all hell?

But in this case, if she shared this burden she was struggling with, the information—if it actually *was* that—would only add to his uneasiness about his grandmother's condition. She definitely didn't want to do that. There were enough things to worry about during the normal course of a procedure without adding this to his stress level.

So she pulled back her lips into a bright smile and shook her head. "No, there's nothing else."

"I'll see you later," he said, turning away. He started to go down the corridor that would ultimately lead him to his grandmother's room.

Dazzling smile not withstanding, Cole couldn't shake the feeling that the perky young doctor was lying to him. But that could just be his imagination. Or, more aptly described, his paranoia. He'd been tense ever since he'd walked in on his grandmother when she was in the throes of one of those "episodes," as she'd referred to the massive palpitations that weakened and all but disabled her. Just like that, the woman he'd always thought of as a pillar of strength threatened to become a mere pile of rubble.

Even now, he couldn't shake the image of her, pale and sweaty, lying on the sofa and almost unable to move. It forced him to see her in a different light. Ericka Baker was a fragile woman. One who wasn't always going to be in his world.

The thought haunted him.

Served him right for breaking his own rules and

growing attached. He'd upbraided himself more than once, but it did no good. The time for taking to the hills had long passed.

The sense of dread anticipation had brought with it was exactly why he was never going to allow himself to grow attached to anyone ever again. Because he knew the ultimate outcome of that attachment.

It was better just to continue to harden his heart and remain alone.

Turning the corner, Cole entered the second room on the right.

His grandmother was sitting up in bed. For a brief moment, she lit up when she saw him. Then, just as quickly, she resumed her role as the somber matriarch of their very small family unit.

"I was beginning to think you'd changed your mind about coming to see me," she pouted.

"How could I?" he asked, brushing his lips against her cheek. "It's the highlight of my day."

"Then you're having a very dull day," she informed him, sitting back against her pillows. She looked at both his hands, which were empty. Her pout intensified.

She asked anyway. "Did you bring me anything decent to eat?"

Instead of answering her, Cole unbuttoned his jacket. Holding the left side open, he extracted a carefully wrapped item from his inner pocket and placed it on the table in front of her.

"Baklava," he announced. "As you requested."

"You really are a joy to me in my old age," Ericka declared, gleefully unwrapping the confection. Taking her first small, dainty bite, she closed her eyes and savored the honeyed confection. For all intents and purposes, she looked as if she was in ecstasy.

Cole pulled over a chair and made himself comfortable, content just to sit and silently watch his grandmother consume, with unabashed pleasure, the dessert he'd smuggled in for her.

He lived in the moment and refused to allow in any thoughts about tomorrow.

Chapter 6

"Don't you ever take a day off?"

Dr. Darel Goodfellow asked the question as he glanced over his shoulder to see who was entering the darkened room. His back was to the door as he reviewed the three x-rays that were currently resting against the screen and backlit to enable better close scrutiny.

Nika flushed. She'd wanted to slip into the small room unobtrusively, but the sliver of light that entered with her made that impossible. She had to admit that she was surprised that the cardiologist was even remotely aware of all the time she'd been putting in. Since she'd come in yesterday on her day off, she was scheduled not to come in today. Heaven knew she needed a day off, but since things were still up in the air as far as Ericka Baker's surgery went, she wanted to be here, rather than in the apartment worrying about the woman.

She wondered if her presence here annoyed Goodfellow

and if she was somehow overstepping her parameters. Her enthusiasm had made her guilty of that more than once.

"I'm sorry, Dr. Goodfellow," she apologized. "I didn't mean to disturb you."

The cardiologist sighed, shaking his head as he looked at the X-rays. "You're not what's disturbing me, Dr. Pulaski."

She didn't like the sound of that.

"Are those Mrs. Baker's X-rays?" She asked the question as a matter of decorum. She knew they were. She'd asked Dr. Allen, the radiologist, if he'd read them yet and was told that they were already with Dr. Goodfellow, who was in the process of studying them in the small, windowless room set aside just for that purpose.

"Yes." Indicating the lineup with a nod of his head, Goodfellow asked, "See anything there that might concern you?"

Her first thought was that he was referring to some anomaly that had to do with Mrs. Baker's heart. After all, that was why the woman was here in the first place. But as she looked at the X-rays, Nika was struck by the appearance of something else.

Her eyes widened as she drew closer for a better look. Her heart began to race. *Not good.*

"Is that...?" Her voice trailed off for a moment as the magnitude of what she was looking at sank in. She raised her eyes to meet Dr. Goodfellow's. "There's a mass in her right breast."

"Yes," the doctor acknowledged very quietly, "there is."

"Is it benign?" she asked hopefully, despite the fact that she knew there was no way to tell without a biopsy.

"*That* is the million-dollar question," Goodfellow replied solemnly. "We're going to have to do a biopsy in order to find out."

She thought of the heart surgery the woman was supposed to have tomorrow. "What about her ablation?"

He shook his head. "That's going to have to be put on hold. Doing a biopsy of the mass takes precedence over the ablation," he informed her.

There was still another matter to take into consideration. Something that interfered with either procedure. "What about Mrs. Baker's elevated blood pressure?"

"That is a complication," the doctor agreed. "But since the mass is rather a large one, I really don't think we have the luxury of sending her home and waiting until the reading is on a more even keel. We need to keep her here and monitor her," he said, thinking out loud. He looked at the center X-ray. "This really doesn't look promising."

Nika always focused on the hopeful aspects, no matter how small. It was what had seen her through more than one unnerving situation. Mentally, she crossed her fingers, hoping that she could get Mrs. Baker to see things that way.

It wasn't going to be easy.

Nika glanced toward the surgeon. "She doesn't know about this yet, does she?"

"*I* didn't know until just a few minutes ago when Jake got the films and brought them to me," he said, referring to the radiologist.

Nika slowly felt the doctor out. Some doctors didn't like including residents in their sessions. "If it's all right with you, doctor, I'd like to be there when you break the news to her."

Darel Goodfellow looked at her in surprise. "Why would you want to do that?" he asked her. "Most of the doctors I know go out of their way *not* to be the one to give a patient what might be tantamount to a death sentence."

Nika fought against the premature assumption. "We don't know for certain that it's malignant yet, Dr. Goodfellow."

After a beat, the doctor inclined his head, as if remembering. He smiled indulgently. "Oh yes, I've almost forgotten what it was like, being new on the job and full of optimism. By all means," he agreed, "you can come along with me when I tell her. You might do her more good than you think."

Nika didn't bother correcting the doctor, but she knew *exactly* what the power of positive thinking could do for a patient. It was the difference between being resigned to die and finding the will to fight.

"Am I going to die?" Ericka Baker asked.

The stoically voiced question broke the eerie silence that immediately ensued after Dr. Goodfellow had informed her of the new complication the X-rays had uncovered. The woman's already ashen complexion seemed to grow just a shade grayer.

"No," Nika answered as the cardiologist searched for the right words that neither asserted nor denied the woman's fears. She faced Mrs. Baker, deliberately avoiding any sort of eye contact with Dr. Goodfellow. She knew she was going out on a limb, but the woman needed to hear these words. "You're not going to die, you're going to fight," she told the noticeably frightened woman. "And just because there's a mass, doesn't automatically mean it's malignant. There's a very good chance that it's benign."

Ericka wanted reassurance, but she was not a fool—she never had been. "I want to hear him say that," she retorted, jerking a thumb at Dr. Goodfellow.

This time Nika made eye contact with the other doctor, silently requesting that the man pick his words carefully and kindly.

"Dr. Pulaski is correct," he finally said. "Until we perform the biopsy, we won't know what we're dealing with. And," he allowed since the woman was obviously waiting for a word of encouragement, "there's a good chance that it's nothing."

"A lot of ruckus for 'nothing,' if you ask me," his patient commented with disgust.

Nika took the woman's thin hand in hers and gave it a gentle squeeze. "You're right, but it's just better to be safe than sorry, Mrs. Baker."

Leaving her hand in Nika's, Ericka looked at her cardiologist. "Could she *be* any more clichéd?" she asked him.

Dr. Goodfellow laughed quietly, clearly amused by the question. "Give her time, Mrs. Baker. She probably will be," he predicted.

Ericka squared her bony shoulders, resigned to what was ahead of her. "So, when do we do it?" she asked, looking from Goodfellow to Nika. "When do we cut into me?"

"I'd like the opportunity to get your blood pressure down a little more first," he told her. "I'm going to authorize keeping you here for observation for a few days while I put you on this blood pressure medication." The cardiologist quickly scribbled the name and dosage instructions on the prescription pad he took out of his breast pocket. Tearing off the sheet, he tucked the pad back into his pocket. "I'll drop it off at the hospital pharmacy for you. We'll see if that doesn't solve the problem."

"The *first* problem," Mrs. Baker emphasized. Her eyes narrowed as she looked at the cardiologist. "And if it doesn't?"

"Then we'll try something else until we find something that works. There're lots of different medications out there," he assured her.

"And meanwhile," she countered grimly, "the cancer's spreading."

"*If* it's cancer," Nika interjected. "Remember, we don't know that it is," she insisted firmly.

But Nika's newest patient looked far from ready to hang on to the life preserver that was being tossed her way.

"Where did you find her, anyway?" she asked Dr. Goodfellow with visible annoyance. "On a cheerleading squad?"

"Might do you a little good to buy into that cheer, Ericka," the doctor pointed out gently. "The mind's a powerful weapon. Don't underestimate it."

"So maybe I'll just wish away the cancer," Ericka proposed sarcastically. It was obvious that she wasn't just angry about this news—she was tired of being under siege.

"There's no proof it's cancer yet," Nika quietly pointed out again.

Ericka sighed deeply and rolled her eyes, but even so, Nika thought she detected a glimmer of hope—and gratitude. She was getting through to the woman, she thought, relieved.

The doctor looked at his watch. "I've got to be going, Mrs. Baker. I'll be by tonight to see how you're doing," he promised.

And with that, he left the room.

Mrs. Baker's eyes shifted to Nika, who was still in the room and gave every indication that she was not about to go anywhere just yet.

"Don't you have to be somewhere else, too?" the woman asked impatiently.

Nika drew the chair closer to Mrs. Baker's bed and sat down. "Actually, no."

Mrs. Baker eyed her suspiciously, clearly not buying what was just said. "They let everyone else in the old bones unit go home?"

"No, everyone in the Geriatrics Unit who was here yesterday is still here today," Nika replied patiently. "I'm off today."

Mrs. Baker looked at her as if she thought the young resident had lost her mind. "Then what the hell are you doing here, breathing in all this stale air?"

"I wanted to find out what your test results were," Nika told her simply.

Mrs. Baker shifted in her bed, moving her thin frame closer to where Nika was sitting. "Why?"

Nika answered her as if it was really self-evident. "Because you're my patient and I'm interested."

Mrs. Baker was silent for a moment as her sharp blue eyes scrutinized her. "How old are you, girl?"

"Thirty." She expected the woman to challenge her, wanting to know how she could be a resident at that age, and Nika was prepared to tell her all about her accelerated course of studies.

But that wasn't what the woman latched on to. "Thirty? And this is the best you can do with your day off?" she shook her head in disbelief and disgust. "Girl, you've got to learn how to live a little."

Nika leaned forward and patted her. "Well, once we get you all better, Mrs. Baker, you can teach me," she told the woman with a gentle smile.

Again the blue eyes seemed to delve right into her as Mrs Baker leaned forward. "You're that sure I'm going to get better?"

"I'm that sure," Nika told her.

Please, God, make me right.

Nika was a firm believer in the good effects of positive thinking, but it didn't always come through a hundred percent of the time.

Ericka sighed and settled back in her bed. "Okay, but if you're wrong, I'm coming back to haunt you."

Nika laughed, delighted by the small display of humor. "It's a deal."

Nika remained in Mrs. Baker's room, talking and doing her best to divert her, until the woman drifted off to sleep. Slipping out, Nika eased the door closed, then turned around and found herself smack up against Cole, who was about to walk in.

Because the door was at her back, Nika had nowhere to retreat to and, for a moment, the hard contours of the detective's body hit against and registered with every part of hers. Reviving very vivid memories of her rescue the other day and summoning a distant, faint ache that pulsed through her body.

For a split second, her breath disappeared. When it returned, she had just enough to blurt out, "Oh, I'm sorry."

Sorrow and regret were the very last emotions that occurred to him. Given a choice, he would have remained exactly where he was, allowing the fleeting, pleasing contact to penetrate further into his consciousness. But for the sake of decorum and because the contact had snaked through to a place he distinctly wanted to remain dormant, he stepped back.

"My fault," he apologized a little stiffly. "I got an early start today," he heard himself explaining, which annoyed him because he made it a point never to have to explain himself. "So I thought I'd look in on my grandmother during my lunch break." He studied Nika closely, as if waiting to be lied to. "How is she?"

"She's sleeping right now," Nika told him, looking at the door.

He'd been a cop long enough to know an evasive answer when he heard one. His green eyes narrowed a little, still watching her intently. "And how is she when she's not sleeping?"

Nika had wanted to be there for Ericka Baker when the doctor had informed the woman about the mass that had shown up on her X-ray. But breaking that information to Mrs. Baker's only living relative was somehow a great deal harder. Harder than she'd imagined.

Still, she couldn't bring herself to just palm him off on Dr. Goodfellow. After all, the man had rescued her. That meant that she owed Detective Baker something more than just giving him the runaround.

Mentally crossing her fingers, hoping for the best, she said, "They found a mass in your grandmother's right breast."

His voice took on a deadly edge. "What kind of mass?"

She took a deep breath. "Hopefully, the benign kind."

He refused to allow himself to dwell on the possibilities if she was wrong. "So what's being done about this 'mass'?" he demanded.

As succinctly as possible, Nika explained what the cardiologist proposed to do—and then went on to tell him why it wasn't being done immediately and hoped that he would understand.

"How long is he going to wait?" Cole's voice was cold, as emotionless as his expression.

About to answer, she quickly stepped to one side as the orderly moved by with a bucket and mop. The stocky man was heading to another room and flashed a sheepish smile at her by way of an apology. He'd all but crashed the bucket into her.

"Not too long," she assured the detective. "Dr. Goodfellow thinks the medicine he's prescribed for her should take care of the problem in a day or so. It's pretty new on the market but it's had some stunning results—"

He dealt in facts. He needed to have facts in front of him to be prepared. "What happens if my grandmother doesn't respond? If her blood pressure stays high? Then what?"

Something told her that even though he'd asked, he really didn't want to hear the answer to that question. Because then he would have to face the possibility. "Why don't we wait and see first? My father used to say there was no point in buying trouble since you could get it for free, anyway."

He looked at her as if she'd just lapsed into a strange language. "What?"

"It loses a little in the translation," she admitted with a laugh. Since he continued to look unenlightened, she explained, "It's an old Polish saying."

Her last name was stitched over the breast pocket of her lab coat. He'd forgotten it. Reading it now, Cole nodded. "Right."

Digging into her pocket, she came up with one card, slightly bent. She held it out to him. "If you have any more questions about your grandmother's condition, or just want to talk, that's my cell number," she told him. She smiled up at him, still holding out the card. "Two ears, no waiting."

With an absent nod, he took the card and pocketed it. "Thanks."

The single word hung in the air as Cole went into his grandmother's room and shut the door behind him.

It was time, she thought, for her to get going. After all, she wasn't really supposed to be here today and since it was her day off, she should try to catch up on a few things she'd been letting go lately. Who knew, the way things were going, when her next day off was going to be?

But before she left, she had one more place to go. She wanted to pay a quick visit to the hospital's morgue to see if anyone had claimed the late Sergeant Kelly's remains.

Making her way through the basement, as she drew near the morgue, she was utterly surprised to catch sight of her uncle.

"Uncle Josef!" she called. When he stopped walking, she quickened her pace to catch up to him. "What are you doing here? Are you lost? You couldn't be here for the food," she teased since the cafeteria was also located in the basement. "Aunt Magda would never forgive you."

"No, I have come here for a more sad reason than eating," he told her. "I come to see if what I am hearing is true." He paused for a moment before saying heavily, "It is."

"What's wrong?" Instantly, she thought of her cousins—and in the next moment, her sisters. Had he come here, looking for her to tell her something? "Has it something to do with the family?" she asked him, almost afraid of the answer because of the expression on his face.

"Yes," he answered. Then, seeing the concern on her face, he added, "But only mine."

"Is it Sasha?" she asked, then, in the next breath, she went through the list of her other cousins' names. "Natalya? Tanya? Kady? Marja?"

He shook his head, his slightly longish gray hair moving back and forth. "No, no, not that family. My blue family."

She stared at him, confused. It took her a moment to understand, only after she remembered that her uncle was a retired police sergeant who'd served proudly with the NYPD.

Her mind leaped to the only conclusion she could. "You're here about Sergeant Kelly?"

The look on her uncle's face told her she'd guessed right before he ever said a word. "Yes, I am here because of him. I am hearing he had nobody. That he is being to lie inside of a drawer of metal. That is not being right," he said with feeling.

It was a small, small world after all. "You were a friend of his?"

"He was teaching me," Josef told her. For a moment, he was back in the past, when his girls were small and he made his living by risking his life every day on the street. "He was my boss. If I am not knowing him, I would not be being here now, talking to you. He was saving my life when I was a rockie," he told her.

"A rookie?" she suggested tactfully.

It was clear that he was frustrated as well as saddened. The former came from having lost touch with the late sergeant after the man had retired from the force. But there was always something to do, jobs to juggle. He was proud of the fact that he had helped all five of his girls through medical school, but it had been at the cost of more than one former friendship.

"Yes, that word. Rookie. I am forgetting the words, but not the feelings. He was being a good man, John was. Good mens should not be being forgotten."

And that was when Nika suddenly realized what her uncle was doing here. "You're claiming his body?" she asked.

Josef nodded his head solemnly. "I am doing what is needing to be done."

"Can I chip in?" she asked. When he looked at her, a slight puzzled expression on his face, she rephrased her question. "Can I give you money toward Sergeant Kelly's funeral?"

His first inclination was to refuse. There was pride involved and the knowledge that funds were tight for her at this stage, but Josef knew that there were some things that a person needed to do. It was a matter of conscience. This he understood.

"That would be being very nice of you," he told her with a grateful smile.

Chapter 7

Nika accompanied her uncle when he went to view the former police sergeant's body. She stood to one side, a silent support for Josef as he paid his last respects to a fellow brother in arms.

"I am sorry we losted touch, my friend. I am hoping you are happy now," he murmured.

As she watched Josef, a thought suddenly occurred to her. And as it did, she felt excitement bubbling up inside of her. So much so that it was a struggle not to say anything while they were in this room, which demanded near silence as well as respect.

Because of her regard for her uncle, Nika let him have his moment and held her tongue until he was ready to leave the hospital morgue.

"Thank you," Josef said to the attendant who'd initially allowed them into the room. "Someone from the funeral place will be coming for him."

Once outside, Nika found herself searching for a way to broach the subject without stomping all over her uncle's grief. It was obvious that he regretted losing touch with the man and she didn't want to intrude on that. At the same time, she really needed to in order to ask him to agree to what she proposed.

How would he feel about her asking him to give his permission to carve up his dead friend so that she could lay her own suspicions to rest? Suspicions that no one else seemed to have?

Walking away from the morgue, Josef abruptly stopped and turned toward her. His eyes were kind as he studied her face. "What is it you are fighting with yourself about, Nika?"

His question caught her completely off guard. She stared at him, stunned. "Excuse me?"

"Something is being on your mind." It wasn't a question. "What is it?"

Mind reading was not a known family trait. To say Nika was flabbergasted was an understatement. "How did you—"

Josef laughed softly, as if the answer was obvious. "I am having five daughters and your aunt Magda. When a woman, she is not talking and it is not because she is sleeping, something is troubling her." His kind eyes delved into hers. "So what is it?"

Okay, here went nothing.

She took a breath and then started. Nika watched her uncle's face carefully as she asked, "Uncle Josef, since you're claiming the sergeant's body, would you request an autopsy?"

Rather than annoyed or upset by the request, her

uncle looked confused. "Why would I want to be doing that?"

She knew how strange this had to sound to him. "Because I really need to know what your friend died from."

"I was told it was heart attack," he said, then asked, "It was not heart attack?"

She had to be honest. "I'm not sure." Glancing around to make sure they weren't going to be overheard, she explained her thinking: that there seemed to be just too many deaths occurring in the ward lately. That, although the sergeant's health could ultimately be regarded as poor, he was being sent back to the nursing home because there was really nothing more to be done for him here at the hospital. This was as good as things were going to be for the former police sergeant.

"So, he was not being healthy," Josef concluded.

She knew what he meant. That the hospital, unable to do anything further for the man, was sending Sergeant Kelly to the nursing home to await death. "No, he wasn't. But it wasn't his heart that was the problem. He had prostate cancer—"

"Your gut, it is talking to you?" Josef surmised knowingly.

She smiled at his phraseology. There was something endearing about it, now that she'd gotten the hang of unraveling its mysteries. "Yes, it is."

Josef nodded, as if accepting the explanation. "Then this is being enough for me," he told her. "You will be having your autopsy, Nika."

Relieved, happy to finally be either confirming her suspicions or laying them to rest, she threw her arms around her uncle's neck and brushed a quick kiss against his cheek.

"Thank you, Uncle Josef!" Slipping her arms from his neck, she said, "I'll get the paperwork started."

It was all just probably her imagination, she reasoned, but until she knew for certain, she wasn't going to be able to have any peace.

And if it *wasn't* just her imagination, she needed to stop whoever or whatever it was that was causing this senseless elimination of senior citizens at their most vulnerable.

Two mornings later, Nika had just begun making her rounds when Shelley, one of the nurses on duty that day, poked her head into the room she was in, simultaneously knocking on the doorjamb to get her attention.

"Dr. Pulaski, Mrs. Silverman just called the nurse's station. She says she wants to see you in her office—her temp office," the heavyset woman added to eliminate any confusion.

All this and heaven, too, Nika thought. But she nodded, saying, "All right, I'll be there as soon as I finish my rounds." Focusing back on her patient, she removed the blood pressure cuff off the man's rail thin arm. Instead of high blood pressure, which was what she was accustomed to running into, this patient's blood pressure was low. So low that there was a risk of the man having hypotension.

Shelley was still in the doorway. The nurse looked somewhat uncomfortable as she relayed the rest of the message. "She said to come *now.*"

Nika pressed her lips together. Why did she feel as if her chain was being yanked by the administrator? Was the woman still upset because of what she'd said the other day? "Did she say why?"

Shelley laughed shortly. "Since when does Mrs. Silverman explain herself?"

Nika hadn't been at the hospital long enough to form a solid opinion based on experience. Just one, again, based on gut feelings.

"From the tone of your voice, never, I'm guessing." And then Nika smiled despite herself. She was beginning to sound like her uncle, bless him.

Momentarily banishing thoughts of the administrator, she looked at the patient in the bed and smiled. "You're doing fine, Mr. Peters. You'll be going home today."

"Home," the man repeated, shaking his bald head. "Wish I could go home."

Despite the order to put in an appearance, Nika lingered with the patient a moment longer. "Why can't you go home?"

The words just poured out as if he'd been damming them up too long. "Because my damn greedy kids sold it out from under me. They said it was for 'the best.' That I couldn't take care of it anymore and that I was better off in a place with people my own age." He snorted with disgust. "Who the hell wants to live with old fossils?" he demanded angrily.

Nika laid a comforting hand on his shoulder, aching for the man. He had to feel as if he'd been cast aside, thrown on a heap and regarded as useless. It wasn't fair.

"I like people your age," she told him kindly. "They have all this knowledge and experience that makes them interesting."

He snorted again, as if what she was saying was just so much make believe. "Maybe, but the only ones I ever seem to meet just want to talk about their last trip to the…bathroom—" the momentary pause gave Nika the impression that Joshua Peters had just cleaned up his language for her sake "—and what happened while they were there."

She had an alternative suggestion for him. "Did you ever think of finding yourself a roommate? The two of you could rent a place together. Kind of like two college students."

Thin shoulders rose and fell helplessly. "I wouldn't know how to get started." But it was obvious that he liked the idea. His eyes lit up. "Would you help me, Doctor?"

Nika grinned. "I thought you'd never ask," she told him, accompanying her words with a wink. "I'll get back to you before you leave today. Don't worry, we'll find a way to get you back on your own again," she promised.

For the first time since she'd seen him admitted a week ago, Joshua Peters grinned and, while the expression didn't transform him to a kid again, it gave her a glimpse of what he must have been like half a century ago when he was in his twenties.

Nika left the room heartened, even though she had a feeling she was going down to be interrogated.

Ella Silverman looked far from happy to see her when Nika walked into the woman's commandeered office. Nika could have sworn she actually saw the icicles forming as the administrator looked her way. "When I said I wanted to see you, Dr. Pulaski, I didn't mean at your leisure."

"Sorry, Mrs. Silverman, I was in the middle of a patient's examination and I couldn't just leave the poor man hanging." Nika dropped into the empty chair before the administrator's desk. That was when she became aware that there was another person in the office with them.

Detective Baker.

What was he doing here? Was he registering a complaint for some reason? She couldn't even begin to form a guess.

So she addressed the administrator instead. "What can I do for you, Mrs. Silverman?"

The other woman looked as if she was in no mood for banter or sarcasm.

"You can cooperate with Detective Baker and answer his questions," she said curtly.

"I wasn't aware that I wasn't cooperating with Detective Baker." She looked at him, wondering why he hadn't come to her instead of taking whatever it was that was bothering him up with the administrator. He didn't strike her as the kind of person who went over people's heads. "Do you have some kind of complaint about the way your grandmother's being treated?"

"This isn't about his grandmother," Ms. Silverman informed her coldly before Cole had a chance to say anything.

Okay, she was now officially confused. Nika looked from the detective to the woman behind the oak desk. "Then what is this about?"

Mrs. Silverman's eyes all but disappeared as she narrowed them. "Do you remember our conversation the other day?"

She remembered being cut down royally. "Vividly," Nika replied.

Mrs. Silverman struggled to maintain her composure. "Well, it seems that one of your unit's deceased, a Philip Mayer, had two children who weren't all that happy with their father dying so suddenly, so they had a private autopsy performed on him."

Every fiber in her body was now alert. "And?" Nika asked, holding her breath.

Ella Silverman's indignation at being put in such a position was barely contained. "And his death was *not* from natural causes."

Yes!

"It wasn't?" Nika tried to keep the excitement from her voice.

"No," Mrs. Silverman practically spat out the word. "The medical examiner discovered a small puncture mark in Mr. Mayer's neck. The M.E. said that it appeared someone had injected air into a major artery." She looked pointedly at Nika. "I'm assuming I don't have to explain the consequences of that to you."

Nika ignored the woman's sarcasm. "Then it *was* a homicide." She refrained from saying, "I told you so," although it wasn't easy. But her gut was right, she thought. Someone was playing Russian roulette with the patients in the Geriatrics Unit.

"It would appear that way." Each word out of the administrator's mouth came grudgingly. The only publicity she wanted for the hospital was of the positive variety. This promised to be the exact opposite, a nightmare in the making. "Detective Baker is going to ask you some questions."

"I'll do anything I can to help," Nika promised as she shifted in her chair in order to face Cole.

"Quite possibly you've already 'helped' too much," Mrs. Silverman informed her angrily.

For a second, Nika didn't understand what the woman was talking about.

And then it hit her. The woman thought she had something to do with the deaths. How? And for God's sake, why?

"Wait a minute," Nika cried. "Am I under suspicion?" How could the administrator even *think* such a thing? "I was the one who brought the unusual number of deaths to your attention, remember?"

The small eyes narrowed. "Exactly. They say that the first one on the scene of a crime usually turns out to be the murderer." The woman's brown eyes shifted toward the detective who had been sent from Homicide to investigate the allegations. "Am I right, Detective Baker?"

There was no emotion in his voice as Cole replied, "If this were a crime novel, yes." He rose from his chair. "I'd like to talk to the doctor in private, please."

"Anything to make this go away as quickly as possible, Detective," the administrator said with forced cheerfulness. "You can use my office," she told him, rising. And then she scowled at Nika again. "I have to speak to our lawyers. The Mayers are threatening a major lawsuit."

Silence hung in the air until Ella Silverman had left the room and shut the door behind her. The second she did, Nika started talking.

"I don't know what she might have said to you, but I *was* the one who brought it to her attention because I was uneasy about the number of people who had recently died in the unit. It didn't seem right. Especially the last one, Sergeant Kelly. He was set to leave the hospital on the day he died."

The moment the last words left her mouth, Nika

realized something. Stunned, she looked at Cole sharply. "Come to think of it, several of the patients died on the day they were supposed to leave. But I am *not* the one responsible for their deaths. I took an oath and it didn't involve killing patients if I couldn't cure them." Her voice filled with passion. "I'm a doctor, for God sakes. My job is to make them better and to keep trying until I finally succeed."

"Are you finished?" Cole asked quietly after a beat.

Nika did her best to try to get a grip on her feelings. "For now," she replied stiffly.

"Good," he replied. "Because I don't see you doing it, either."

Bracing herself for what she felt was the inevitable round two, she was pulled up short. Nika blinked. "You don't?"

"No."

He studied her for a long moment. The stare was known to cause people with guilty consciences to start confessing. His grandmother's attending physician, he noted, merely returned his gaze.

The only thing she was guilty of, he concluded, was invading his imagination and raising his body temperature every time he thought of that trim, supple body climbing over his.

"Should I?" he asked mildly.

"No!" Realizing she was all but shouting, Nika lowered her voice. "I mean, the thought is so ridiculous I don't see why it even has to be addressed——"

"It has to be addressed," he informed her, his tone still without any emotion, "because everyone is supposed to be a suspect until they're cleared. But don't worry—I already asked around. You were with my grandmother when Sergeant Kelly suffered his so-called heart attack. So unless you can do it by remote control, that pretty much puts you in the clear. Besides, I've seen you with my grandmother. You're not the killing type. Anyone who'd go out of their way to catch a spider in order to set it free wouldn't kill another human being."

Their eyes met. She knew that he hadn't been there when she'd removed the spider from his grandmother's room. Mrs. Baker's alarmed cry had brought her hurrying into the woman's room, only to discover that there was a spider crawling across the blanket at the foot of her bed.

Mrs. Baker had expressed surprise when, instead of killing the spider, she'd opened the window and allowed the "intruder" to glide out on a breeze. She'd obviously relayed the incident to him.

Nika breathed a sigh of relief. "Thank you."

"Just following the evidence," he told her simply. "But someone apparently did kill Mr. Mayer, and by your own admission you seem to believe that he's not the only one. Who else do you think was killed—and why?"

"I can get a printout of the deaths that have taken place in the last twelve months in the Geriatrics Unit and give it to you. As to why—" Nika raised and lowered her shoulders, the motion echoing the helpless feeling she had when it came to an explanation or a motive. "I have no idea."

"Well, the list's a start." And maybe she was wrong. He'd rather believe that than think that there was a homicidal maniac running around loose in the hospital, especially since G was here. "I'm also going to want a list of anyone who's died while in the hospital in the last year."

Her eyes widened. "You think it's gone beyond just the Geriatrics Unit?"

"Maybe, maybe not. The second list can be our control group until proven otherwise." He took a breath, then asked a question that was far more personal. "By the way, how *is* my grandmother doing?"

She knew he'd been to see the woman last night, so what he was asking for was an update as of this morning. Something she wasn't able to give him yet. "I was just about to check on her this morning when I was summoned down here."

"Well then, let's get you back to your floor," he suggested.

She was all for that. "Oh, I think you should know," she began as they walked to the elevator, "my uncle claimed Sergeant Kelly's body and he agreed to request an autopsy."

"What's your uncle's connection to Kelly?" Cole asked.

"My uncle said Kelly trained him when he came on the force. The man doesn't seem to have anyone. So many of the people in the Geriatrics Unit don't," she added. "It's really very sad. You live your whole life working, thinking you're making a difference, and in the end, it's like nobody noticed."

They reached the elevator bank. Cole looked at her for a long moment. "That's pretty pessimistic for you."

So he had been paying attention, she thought, a smile springing to her lips. "Just an observation. Anyway, I told Uncle Josef what I suspected. Until now, there've been no autopsies. The bodies were either claimed by family and buried, or the city stepped in and had them cremated. Mrs. Silverman wouldn't allow me to voice my suspicions and try to get someone to give us permission to exhume a body.

"When my uncle came to claim Kelly's remains, I thought it was a chance to find out if anything was actually going on, or if all this was just a horrible set of coincidences. I was hoping for the latter, but I couldn't just go on not knowing. I have an obligation to protect my patients from *any* harm." She paused, waiting for him to say something.

Cole had begun to wonder if she was ever coming up for air. "Have you always been such a crusader?" The elevator arrived and they got on. Reaching past her to push the button, he realized that she'd become rigid.

Probably remembering the other day, he thought. He debated reassuring her that the odds of having the elevator get stuck again so soon in the same building were incredibly small, but he decided to let it go. She was smart enough to figure it out for herself. The woman, he noted almost against his will, was pretty much a total package: brains and looks. That didn't happen very often.

"Actually," she was saying, "my mother always thought of me as a rebel."

"Really?" He couldn't readily envision her in that role. She was far too much of a do-gooder. "And what is it you rebelled against?"

Nika smiled. "My mother."

Her unexpected answer made him laugh.

Nika found herself warming to the sound. There was something deep and rich in his laughter and if she hadn't known better, she would have said it wrapped itself around her.

"Sounds pretty normal to me," he told her. And

normal, he added silently, was to be envied. "So tell me more about your suspicions."

The doors opened on the first floor and several people came in. Nika and Cole moved to the back of the car, but they were still crowded, pushed up against one another. She could feel her body tingling in response. She stole a side glance, wondering if he felt anything as well. Probably not.

"What do you want to know?"

He felt her drawing in a breath. Felt her body move against his and realized it was making more of an impression on him than it should have. What *was* it about this woman that kept getting to him? "For starters, when did you start having these suspicions?"

"Just with the last death," she confessed.

Why was she having this trouble concentrating? They were in an elevator, for God sakes. With a whole bunch of other people. Why did her skin insist on tingling like this? She forced herself to concentrate on her answer to his question.

"It didn't feel right to me. Then I remembered that we'd just lost someone a little more than two weeks ago. And there was a death the first day I came to work in this unit. I remember how hopeless it left me feeling until I snapped out of it. So I started going through the files of all the people who'd recently died in the unit. I kept going back, hoping what I saw as a trend was actually just a fluke. But it wasn't. And the number was a lot higher than the national average."

The elevator doors opened on two and, while one person got off, three others got on. Nika was forced to move even closer into Cole. It didn't go unnoticed by either of them.

Their eyes met and held and, for a moment, everything else faded away.

Cole forced his mind back on the topic. "The dead people had a lot going against them," he told her in a low voice as he pointed out the obvious. "They were old, they were sick, otherwise they wouldn't have been here, and there are more deaths among old people than in any other age bracket."

"I know all that," she insisted. "But I had this gut feeling—"

"A gut feeling," he repeated. By now, he was whispering the words into her ear because there were too many people around.

"Yes." She said the word defiantly, waiting for him to make fun of it and her. Instead, she was aware of him nodding his head. And acutely aware of the way his breath touched the side of her face. She could feel her stomach muscles contracting.

"I've always had the utmost respect for gut feelings," he told her.

Nika struggled to keep the sound of his voice from completely blotting out everything else.

Had to be the effect of riding in a crowded elevator, she silently insisted.

Or hoped.

Chapter 8

Taking the long, slender hand in both of his, Cole stood on one side of his grandmother's hospital bed and asked, "How are you today, G?"

Though it was muted, it was difficult to miss the affection in his voice. Difficult, too, to miss the disappointment that washed over his features when he realized that his grandmother was looking at him blankly, as if she was trying to place who he was.

And then the fog must have lifted from her brain, because in the next moment Ericka Baker smiled at her grandson, however fleetingly.

It took longer for the detective's features to relax. His grandmother's dance with dementia, however temporary those moments were, was hitting him hard, even though he said nothing.

These two were people, Nika guessed, who were part

of a world where affection wasn't demonstrated, it was simply a given. And understood.

"Restless," his grandmother replied to his question. "How else would I be, sitting around and waiting?" The older woman looked at Nika. "How much longer do I have to stay here?"

"You're going to make me feel that you don't like my company, Mrs. Baker," Nika said as she secured the blood pressure cuff on the woman's arm. Assured it was fastened, she began to inflate it.

"I have a life to get back to," Ericka responded sharply. She looked pointedly at her grandson, obviously seeking an ally. "And I've got canasta games waiting to be played. God knows the maid probably stripped the entire house and sold everything by now."

"You have a maid?" Nika watched as the arrow on the gauge kept rising. "I'm impressed."

"It's a housecleaning service," Cole told her. "Matilda comes by every two weeks to clean. She's been doing that for the last ten years," he said, trying to make his grandmother admit that the woman was incredibly trustworthy.

"She has nothing to clean," Mrs. Baker told her proudly. "I keep a spotless house. You're wasting your money, Coleman."

This was an old argument. "I wouldn't be if you let her do her job and stop trying to outdo her, G," he replied patiently.

Ericka raised her chin. She was nothing if not a woman of old-fashioned values. "A woman who can't clean her own house doesn't deserve one."

"You really should let Matilda do her job," Nika advised, deflating the cuff again. "It'll make your grandson feel as if he's finally able to help you, for a change. You know, paying you back for all the times you were there for him."

Ericka Baker looked from her attending physician to her grandson. Had there been no noise, Nika was fairly certain she would have been able to hear the wheels turning in the woman's head. And grinding to an abrupt halt.

Her eyebrows touched as she narrowed her eyes. "You've been telling her about us, boy?"

"I'm your attending physician, Mrs. Baker," Nika reminded her before Cole had a chance to say anything. "I ask questions, he answers. It's all confidential," she assured the woman. "Meant strictly for patient history."

Ericka tossed her head. "I'm the patient. Talk to *me* about my history," she instructed.

Nika shook her head with a laugh. "You are a pistol, Mrs. Baker."

"And she doesn't shoot blanks," Cole warned with just a hint of a smile. He noticed that his grandmother seemed to preen at the warning.

Despite the conversation, his grandmother didn't lose sight of what was really important to her. "So? How is it?" the older woman wanted to know. "My blood pressure. Is it low enough for you yet?"

Nika replaced the cuff where it belonged. "Not yet, but we're getting closer."

Ericka scowled. "How much are they paying you to keep my body in this bed?" she wanted to know.

Nika bit her lower lip to keep from laughing. She knew Ericka would take offense. "Not nearly enough, trust me. And if you're curious, your blood pressure is 146 over 95."

Ericka tilted her head, weighing the numbers. "It's been higher. Isn't that low enough for you?" she demanded.

Nika knew the woman was trying to intimidate her. *Sorry, Mrs. Baker, I cut my teeth on Ella Silverman. And Mama.* "I'm afraid it has to be lower." Her tone was firm.

Mrs. Baker frowned and looked up at her grandson. "You had to get me a stubborn doctor? You couldn't pull a more easygoing one out of the elevator?" she asked.

Nika laughed at the question. "Luck of the draw, I'm afraid. I was the only one in the elevator at the time." When she glanced in his direction, she saw that the detective was studying her. Their eyes met for the briefest of moments. Tiny shivers raced up and down her spine.

"I think she's very good for you, G," Cole told his grandmother, his voice low, patient. "She's not afraid of you. That's a plus."

Ericka sighed and then waved him out. "Go, do your police work. Be a detective. I don't need you here if you're not going to back me up."

He laughed and kissed Ericka's forehead. Nika found that the sound seemed to burrow right into her. She was going to have to find a way to block that. She was far too old to be reacting like a teenage girl with her first major crush.

"See you later, G," Cole promised.

"You bet you will," she called after him. "They'll probably shackle me to the bed next!"

Nika left the room with him, easing the door closed behind her. The sound of his grandmother's voice followed them out.

"How much longer do you think it'll be before she

can have that biopsy?" he asked once they were outside in the corridor.

The blood pressure readings were going down, but not fast enough to suit any of them, Nika thought. She fully sympathized with their frustration. "At this rate, hopefully a week."

The news didn't please him. "That long? Will her insurance cover her staying here for that amount of time?"

"With the right reports filed and the extenuating circumstances spelled out, yes." She knew how iffy the health insurance world was. Apparently, so did he. "If not, Patience Memorial has provisions for senior citizens and people who don't have any health insurance to begin with." She flashed him an encouraging smile. "Don't worry, it'll be taken care of," she promised him. And then she remembered what they had talked about prior to going to Ericka's room. "Meanwhile, I need to get you that list."

At the moment, Cole had several cases pending. With his partner down and out with the flu—it had hit the man late yesterday, according to the phone call he'd gotten this morning—it felt as if his work had suddenly tripled on him rather than just doubled.

"You don't have to get it this second," he told her. "Why don't I pick it up when I swing by to see my grandmother tonight?"

That sounded good to her. So did seeing him again. God, she really was acting like an adolescent, she thought, even as she nodded.

"It's a date—" Nika stopped abruptly, realizing what she'd just said. "I mean…" Her voice trailed off as she hunted for a way to gracefully backtrack from the slip.

She kind of looked cute, flustered like that, he

thought. Taking pity, he came to her rescue. "I know what you mean, Doctor," he said, getting her off the hook. "Besides," he added, "that isn't an entirely bad idea."

He wasn't sure which of them was more surprised to hear that, her or him. The words had just slipped out.

Nika stared at him. Was the detective actually asking her out? Had she missed something just now? "It's not?"

He liked the way her eyes widened when she was surprised. Liked, he found himself admitting, the whole package that comprised the young, eager doctor. After all, he wasn't made of stone. Only his heart was. But he found he did just fine without involving it, in the scheme of things.

"No law says that there can't be food around when you give me your input about the deceased patients," he told her. "I'm assuming that the patients were your patients."

"The last few were, yes. Before that I was just helping out on the floor whenever I had the chance." She could see by the puzzled look on his face that she was going to have to explain that. "Initially, they had me working in the E.R. when I came here. They break everyone in on the E.R. The thinking behind that is that if you don't run screaming into the night after a rotation in the E.R., you have at least some of what it takes to become a dedicated doctor."

And she was dedicated, he noticed. It was evident in everything she did. It also meant that his grandmother was in good hands.

Glancing at his watch, he realized he had to be getting back. "All right, I'll meet you here after six." It occurred to him that he was making assumptions. "Will you be off by then?"

She nodded. "Barring an act of God, yes."

"Let's hope God's busy with something else, then," Cole commented just before he took his leave.

He didn't realize he was smiling until he caught his reflection in a dormant monitor as he passed it. Cole pulled his features into a somber expression.

"Why Geriatrics?"

Cole tendered the question over a house salad and sesame-flecked breadsticks as he and his grandmother's incredibly enthusiastic physician waited for their main course.

Mt. Vesuvius was a small restaurant that had been part of the neighborhood for the last three decades. It barely accommodated the fourteen tables that were vying for space on the sawdust-covered floor. But the aroma, comprised of a host of different herbs and spices, that filled the area was the stuff that dreams and expanding waistlines were made of.

"I like hearing stories," she told him frankly.

Cole tried to make sense of her answer in the present context and couldn't. "Excuse me?"

Nika broke off a piece of the breadstick and popped it into her mouth, then explained. "Old people are filled with experiences, with stories they're dying to share with someone. Most of their families are too busy earning a living or trying to squeeze the last drop of life out of their existences. They don't have the time to listen to them."

"And you have time?" he questioned with only the smallest sliver of sarcasm. She was a doctor, one of the busiest, most demanding professions on the planet—outside of homicide detective. His guess was that time was not a commodity that she had in great supply.

"I can multitask very efficiently," Nika said with a grin. "And most of the time, my ears aren't doing anything except hanging around anyway. So I listen to them, and get just as much as I give—sometimes more. There's a lot of untapped wisdom to be gotten from those old people," she assured him.

He watched her polish off the rest of the breadstick. "I can see why my grandmother likes you."

Nika was surprised by his comment. And pleased. "She told you that?"

"No, not in so many words," he admitted. "But I know her. I can see it in her eyes, in the way she talks to you. In the way she talks *about* you. When I visit her, she doesn't spend the entire time telling me everything you did wrong, which she would if she didn't like you."

Nika laughed. "Now you're going to give me performance anxiety."

He watched her for a long moment. So long that her stomach had time to tighten and then flutter restlessly not once, but twice. "I'm sure you perform very well," he told her, his voice low.

After a beat, Nika realized that she had to tell herself to breathe.

She was relieved when she saw the waitress approaching with their orders. "Dinner's here," she told him needlessly.

They spent the next forty-five minutes discussing the list she'd given him and deliberately ignoring the electricity that had shown up and taken a seat at the table between them. The electricity that crackled sharply and unexpectedly not once, but several times during the course of the meal and the dessert that followed.

The electricity, she thought, that would wind up tripping her up. If she was going to fall hard for somebody—and so far she hadn't in all her thirty years—Cole Baker was the wrong man to pick. He was good to his grandmother and handy to have around when elevators died, but she had a feeling that he would neither want nor know what to do with a woman's heart if it was offered to him.

"The odd thing was," Nika continued as the busboy cleared away their plates, "I didn't realize until I reviewed the names on the list that there were several patients who lived in either a nursing home or in an assisted living facility. They were the patients who either had no family or whose families felt that, by setting them up in these homes, their obligation to show up in their lives from time to time was rescinded.

"Those are the people, who don't understand the meaning of the phrase, 'the ties that bind,'" she continued, unaware that her voice was swelling with passion. "They just want to appease their consciences."

He looked down the list, which he had placed next to his plate. "What about the other names? Anything strike you as similar there as well?"

"Yes," she said grimly. Something else had occurred to her after she'd printed the list up. "Every one of them had a disease that was not about to be cured."

He made the natural assumption. "They were terminal, then?"

"They were terminal," she echoed. "Some of them were in the late stages of cancer, of leukemia, of Parkinson's disease. The sad thing is," she continued, "for the most part, the cancer patients could have been cured if they'd only come in sooner. But for one reason or another, they had hoped that their symptoms would just go away and that they'd be all right again."

She sighed. It was such a waste. "It doesn't work like that. And, in this day and age, it seems a shame that these people don't take advantage of all the advances that medicine has made." She gave him an example. "One of the patients, a Mrs. Ida Jones, was too embarrassed to tell her doctor that she was having pains around her pelvic area." Reaching over to the paper, she tapped the fourth line. "She's the fourth name on the list."

Cole looked down at the printout. She had included the addresses, as well as thumbnail descriptions of the initial complaint that the patients had come in with, and the presumed cause of death that had ultimately seen them out. At first glance, it all appeared perfectly acceptable to him.

But obviously it wasn't. Not if one of Patience Memorial's own attending physicians was suspicious that something more was going on than readily met the eye.

Cole scanned the names again. "You said that some of these patients had no families."

"Right. Most of the ones who were brought in from the local nursing homes had no next of kin to contact," she repeated. "When they died, the hospital notified the head administrator at the homes." She hated how sad that sounded.

Since the records were all here, in the interest of time he decided to attempt a shortcut. "Do you think you can get me the names of the next of kin for the others?"

Mrs. Silverman would probably have her head—and

her job—if she found out. But Silverman was not her concern. These former patients were.

"No problem," she assured him. The man in Records owed her a favor. "I take it you want to talk to them."

He nodded. While they'd been having dinner, one of the waiters had approached each table and lit the thick, chunky candles that were in the center. The candlelight seemed to love her. It took him a second to get his mind back on her question.

"I thought I'd see if there were any unusual life insurance policies involved."

She hadn't thought of that. That made it so callous. "You think this is about money?"

At this point, he didn't know. He was casting out lines to see if he could get a nibble.

"Stranger things have happened," he told her. "There was a case several years ago where two retired schoolteachers were taking out large insurance polices on homeless vagrants in the area. They'd get them to sign the papers in exchange for a hot meal and some clean clothes. After a certain amount of time had passed, they would run the poor sap down in their car and kill him in order to collect the money. They took turns," he added, shaking his head.

Nika stared at him, numbed by the blatant horror of what he was telling her. "You're kidding," she whispered incredulously.

"That's not the kind of headline that jokes are made about," he told her.

It made him sick to his stomach to recall the case. The retired schoolteachers had been in their early seventies. Schoolteachers, for God sakes. They were the very ones involved in helping to mold the nation's children and their moral character.

"My point," he continued, "is that maybe someone is taking out polices on these people, then killing them off so that they can collect."

Put that way, she supposed that it did sound plausible. "The M.E. found a small puncture wound in Mr. Mayer's neck," she said, repeating what they both knew, then extrapolating on it. "If that's the method of killing them off, and it is pretty simple and very effective—no muss, no fuss, not even any drugs to get and possibly leave a trail—then I'm guessing the same person would be paying a "visit" to all the other patients just before they died."

"Sounds right." He leaned forward, watching her. Watching the way light played off the soft contours of her face. "What are you driving at?"

"We have a number of surveillance cameras on the floor." She hoped she wasn't insulting him by pointing that out. "Maybe we'll get lucky and the same face will keep popping up on the tapes—provided that hospital security hangs on to the tapes for more than a month at a time," Nika qualified.

He looked at her, finding that he had to suppress a smile. Not exactly something he needed to do on a regular basis. He'd been thinking the same thing, but rather than mention that to her, he decided to allow the doctor to bask in the feeling that she was making headway in the case for him.

"I'm impressed," he told her. "You think like a cop. Anyone in your family on the force?"

Directly, no, but she was now part of an extended family, so technically, the answer was yes. "Three of my cousins are married to law enforcement officers. My uncle used to be a police sergeant on the NYPD and now runs a security firm with another one of his sons-in-law. As a matter of fact, the hospital contracts his firm for extra help around the holidays, and whenever anyone of major importance comes to the hospital to have a procedure performed."

A thought struck her. "Uncle Josef would probably be able to get those tapes for you a lot faster than if you went through regular channels."

His "channels" usually involved tersely voiced orders issued to underlings, but for now, Cole kept that to himself. She was enjoying herself too much "helping." Right now, it cost him nothing to allow her to go on thinking she was an asset.

"That would be very helpful," he agreed. "You're a very handy person to have around, Dr. Pulaski."

That was way too formal for a man who was making her skin tingle on a regular basis. "You yanked me out of the jaws of a paralyzed elevator—I think you should call me by my first name." She'd already told him once, but she had a feeling he'd probably forgotten it. "It's Nika."

"Nika?" he repeated, a little amused and bewildered by the name at the same time. "Is that your whole name?"

She shook her head. "It's short for Veronika," she told him. "But nobody calls me that." They all found it much too formal and she was not that way, Nika added silently.

"Veronika." He rolled the name over on his tongue, as if appraising it for taste and texture. "Then I'll be the first," he told her.

He probably would be, she thought, but she wasn't

thinking about her name. Instead, she was focused on the wave of anticipation that had suddenly risen up, riding the tide of adrenaline within her that absolutely refused to subside no matter how hard she tried to bank it down or smother it.

She'd never been this attracted to a man before. She had a feeling she was going to pay for that.

Chapter 9

When the waiter brought the check over and placed it on the table in front of Cole, Nika opened her purse and began rummaging through it.

Watching her for a moment, Cole asked, "What are you doing?"

"Looking for my wallet so I can pay my share of the bill," she answered, sparing him a look just before she located her elusive wallet, which had sunk to the bottom of her purse, and took it out.

"You don't have a share," he replied. When she seemed confused, he said, "I used the D-word, remember?"

Nika's confusion lingered for another couple of seconds before dissipating, and when it did, she was still a little surprised because she hadn't really thought he'd meant it at the time.

"You said date," she recalled.

He took out his own wallet. "It's coming back to you," he observed, nodding his head in approval. She had no idea if he was serious or pulling her leg. "Good. I was beginning to think that I imagined the whole conversation."

She wasn't comfortable with this. Did he think she was too poor to pay her own way? She was almost certain that this wasn't really a date. "I'd still like to pay my half."

Cole remained firm and shook his head. "Not going to break me," he commented. "Besides, I don't have staggering student loans to pay back."

Was that why he was paying for dinner? Pity? He needed to be set straight. "Neither do I."

A glimmer of surprise was evident in his eyes. "I thought all medical students came out of school with huge debts."

Usually, they did. But she and her sisters were very lucky that way. "My mother had an older sister, Zofia, who was an actuary at one of the major insurance companies. She worked all of her life, and then died without enjoying any of her money. She left it to my mother, who used it to put all of us through school." Wielding it like a weapon, she added silently, remembering her mother's non-negotiable terms. They could only get their educations paid for if they agreed to become doctors. Luckily, that turned out to be exactly what they wanted, except for perhaps the baby, Henryka, who took a while to come around.

Cole wasn't about to accept defeat. He had another card to play. "All right, then let me fall back on my male ego. You pay, it'll be bruised." He leaned in closer to her across the table. "If I called this a business dinner, would that make you feel less like you were compromising whatever ideals are keeping you from allowing me to pay for this?"

"It's not that, it's—business?" Nika abruptly asked, the homicide detective's choice of words suddenly sinking in.

Cole nodded. "You can think of yourself as my informant."

She had a feeling that she might have just met her match, as far as stubbornness went. Cole sounded as if he would go on arguing with her until she finally gave in. Better sooner than later. Besides, this was only a minor point. She just didn't want him to feel he *had* to pay for her.

"All right," she allowed with a smile of indulgence. "To save your ego."

"Good," he accepted her explanation. Rather than using a credit card, Cole placed several bills on the tab, more than covering the cost of their dinners as well as adding a healthy-size tip. "Ready?" he asked.

Picking up her purse, Nika slipped her wallet back into it and then echoed, "ready," just as she began to rise to her feet.

She was caught off guard when Cole circled the table and came up behind her, drawing the chair away so that she didn't have to push it back. Nika looked at him over her shoulder, an uncertain expression on her face.

He laughed when he caught a glimpse of it. "Don't worry, I'm not about to trip you or do something strange." He moved the chair back in as she stepped to one side. "Haven't you ever had anyone treat you like a lady?"

The answer required no thought on her part. "Not recently."

"Then you've been seeing the wrong kind of men," he concluded.

"The only kind of men I've been seeing since I arrived in New York have either been bleeding, throwing up or are contagious."

The woman was talking about work. Placing his hand to the small of her back, Cole guided her around the tables, now all filled, and toward the front door. As he walked past the receptionist's tall, narrow desk, he nodded goodbye.

Nika caught the silent exchange and wondered how well he knew the woman—was he a regular customer, or was there something more to it—and why did that even matter? she asked herself in the next thought.

"Are you telling me you haven't gone out socially since you got here?" he asked her.

She saw no reason to be cagey. After all, it wasn't as if this was an *actual* date. He'd just been kidding when he'd said that.

"I'm telling you I haven't gone out, period. Except to Uncle Josef's a couple of times." And even that had an obligation attached to it. "Turning up at my uncle and aunt's table in Queens every so often is mandatory." There was a note of fondness in her voice as she referred to the couple. "If I miss that, one or both of them come looking for me."

He held the door open for her. "You don't sound like you mind."

She didn't. None of them did even though a couple of her cousins pretended to grumble about it on occasion just for form's sake. "It's nice having family," she told him. "A bigger family," she amended. Nika walked right past his car, which was parked in a prime spot at the curb.

"Hey, where are you going?" he asked, calling her attention to the vehicle.

She stopped walking, but didn't retrace her steps. She saw no reason for that. "To the bus stop. My sister Alyx has the car, because she's got the third shift at the hospital," she explained, citing why she wasn't going back to the hospital to pick up the communal car they all shared.

"Where do you live?" he wanted to know. "I'll take you home."

That was going above and beyond the call of duty, she thought. Nobody should have to buck New York traffic if they didn't have to.

"You don't have to go out of your way. I'm used to taking buses and trains," she told him. "Reminds me of home—Chicago," she elaborated.

Cole shook his head. "Is everything an argument with you?" he asked.

She hadn't meant it to sound like an argument. "No, I just didn't want to be any trouble."

"You're more trouble when you argue," he told her, beckoning her over. "Now, unless you live in Virginia, taking you to your apartment isn't going to be out of my way."

"No, it's not as far away as Virginia," she said, giving in. She did a quick mental review. "Actually, it's only about a little more than a mile away. On a nice day, I walk."

"So I take it you haven't done much walking, then," he quipped. Pointing his key at his vehicle, he pressed down on one of the indentations, releasing the security system. The locks popped open, accompanied by a beep. "If we're lucky, there's about two decent days in New York City, weather-wise. One day comes in the spring and the other day comes in the fall."

Nika opened the door on the passenger side. "You don't like New York?" she asked, getting in.

"I love New York," he contradicted, getting in on the driver's side, then closing the door. "It's the weather I hate. It's always either too humid, too rainy, too cold, too something." Cole glanced to see if she'd put on her seat belt. Satisfied that she had, Cole started up the car. "And your address?" he prodded.

She realized that she hadn't given it to him and rattled it off. With a nod of his head, he backed out of the space.

And got all of about five feet before he queued his car into the slow drip of traffic. From what he could see, it appeared to be bumper-to-bumper. Probably was all the way from the restaurant to the building where she lived.

She made the same assessment. "I can get out and walk from here," Nika volunteered cheerfully.

"I said I was taking you home, so I'm taking you home," he told her. "Besides, I'm going to be stuck in this traffic whether you're in the car or not, so you might as well keep me company."

"If you put it that way—"

"I do."

"Then, okay." She studied his profile for a moment, her eyes drifting over the hard, rigid lines that comprised the planes and angles of the man's face.

It was a noble face, she decided. Not soft, but noble. The kind of face a victim of a crime could trust. While it was evident that he wasn't running the danger of having someone accuse him of being warmth personified, the detective did give off an aura of strength, of dedication and competence. That would be the kind of policeman she would want to turn to if she found herself ever needing one.

Cole could feel her eyes on him. Could feel her scrutinizing him as he was driving. Did he measure up? he wondered.

"What?" he finally asked. "Is there sauce on my face or something?" The next moment, since they were now at a complete standstill, Cole angled the rearview mirror so he could see his reflection for himself.

"No, I was just thinking. You're not nearly as hardnosed as you initially came off," she told him. And before he could comment or deny her assessment, she added, "I'm glad."

She sounded positively cheerful as she made the pronouncement. He hadn't thought that women like her existed. "Why?"

"Because it makes you easier to talk to." And then she got to the more important reason. "And because someone else might not have believed me when I said that I was innocent."

He wasn't about to take credit where none was due. "I already told you, you had an alibi for the time that Sergeant Kelly was killed. I'm not the kind of detective who ignores the facts just because they don't fit in with my theory."

"And," she continued, "you took it upon yourself to look into my alibi—an alibi I didn't even know I needed—before I ever said anything."

He shrugged away her gratitude. "It's called being a good detective."

In her book, it was called more than that. He could have made her life miserable if he'd wanted to, putting the burden of proof on her shoulders. "All the same, I'm glad you're on my side."

"I don't take sides," he corrected her, "I follow the evidence."

She refused to accept that. Nika shook her head. "Too late to be Mr. Gruff-and-Cold," she informed him brightly. "I've seen your soft underbelly, Detective Baker, and I know who you are."

He cleared his throat and looked straight ahead at the clogged streets before him. Compliments had always made him uncomfortable. Especially undeserved ones. He knew what he was and it didn't involve being a saint, or a knight in shining armor. His armor had long since rusted.

"I suggest you stop getting into the pharmacy supply closet," he told her matter-of-factly.

Nika nodded as if he'd said something serious. "I'll put it on my 'not to do' list," she promised.

He could hear the smile in her voice and, for some reason, although he was determined not to let it, it still managed to seep in under his skin and spill out to his very core.

"You don't have to get out," Nika told him when they were finally within view of her apartment building. She pointed out the structure on the right. At the same time, she got the feeling he wasn't about to listen to her. "You'll lose your spot in the flow of traffic," she warned.

Cole angled the vehicle's way out of the line of traffic and drove toward the building's underground parking structure.

"That isn't flow," he said with a touch of disgust. "That doesn't even qualify as a drip. Maybe it'll get better when I get back." Although he didn't hold out too much hope.

"Back from where?" she asked.

Driving into the structure, Cole glanced up to see if there were any signs pointing out the way to guest parking. Finding them, he drove his car toward the designated area.

Several spaces were unoccupied. He took the first he came to. He'd never been one to see the point of jockeying for a position that amounted to being just a few feet closer to his destination. He liked walking. He liked leaving his car dent-free even more.

"Back from bringing you up to your door," he told her as he slipped into the space.

She didn't know whether to be amused or a little nervous. She realized that she was both. "You are taking the D-word seriously, aren't you?" she asked, unbuckling her seat belt.

"I'm taking the city seriously," he countered. Getting out, he rounded the trunk and was at her door in time to open it for her. "Single women shouldn't be roaming around by themselves at night. Especially if they're young and attractive."

He said it so matter-of-factly, she almost missed the compliment. But it echoed back to her in her mind, causing her to smile.

Whether he realized it or not, he'd just told her he thought she was attractive. Nika grinned.

"*Really* not as gruff as you want people to think you are," she repeated.

Hiking her purse strap onto her shoulder, she led the way to the elevator.

"Just carrying out the *protect* portion of my job description," he told her. Reaching the elevator a step before she did, he pressed for the car.

This was above and beyond the call of duty, as far as she was concerned, but if he didn't want any attention drawn to that, it was fine with her. "Whatever you say."

Cole raised an eyebrow as he heard the amusement in her voice. He realized that she wasn't buying into his story any more than he was. He'd been trying to tell himself that he was just bringing a potential witness home, nothing more. And that she *wasn't* a woman who had somehow managed, in an unbelievably short amount of time, to work her way under his skin when he wasn't looking. Moreover, she'd also managed to make him start wondering what it would be like to relate to another human being on some level other than as a cop working a case.

Dangerous ground, he warned himself.

None of the words, silent though they were, were making any sort of an impression on him.

This wasn't good, he thought.

They got on the elevator and, for the moment, they had it to themselves. As soon as the doors closed, the inside of the car began to fill up with a scent that was vaguely familiar and teased his less than lucid memory banks, challenging them to recall what it was.

Vanilla? Lavender?

He couldn't quite place the scent but he did know that it was familiar. And that he liked it. It stirred things on some semi-faraway region in his soul that hadn't been functioning lately—or, more truthfully, hadn't been functioning for a very, very long time.

The elevator, for once, turned out to be an express, taking them from the basement straight to her floor.

The doors slid open on five.

"This way," Nika told him, getting off the elevator. She turned to the right immediately, taking him down a long, modernly decorated hallway.

Cole walked beside her until she stopped before 5E. The apartment next to hers, 5F, was still empty, she thought absently. Alyx had told her all about the murder that had taken place there before she'd arrived in the city.

She did her best not to think about it.

Apparently the superintendent was having trouble renting it out now. Nobody wanted to live in a place where someone had been killed. The supposed "vibrations," coupled with vivid imaginations, were just too much to handle for the potential renters who'd come to look the apartment over so far. She had to admit she couldn't say she blamed them.

"Well, this is it," she told him, nodding toward the door as she turned around to face him. Without looking into the yawning abyss that was her purse, Nika began to rummage through it with her hand, searching for the familiar shape of her house keys. "You've brought me to my door, so you are now officially relieved of duty," she teased.

He had to get going, Cole thought. Nika had already told him that she was going to see about filling in some of the information he'd requested earlier. But that didn't mean he couldn't put someone at the precinct to work on the project as well. There was a chance that the computer wizard he used would come up with more data than Nika had at her disposal. At the very least, one set of information could wind up augmenting the other.

It only made sense.

What didn't make sense was why he wasn't moving away. He should be taking his leave and just going. Instead, he stood there, looking at her, thinking that he'd looked down into prettier faces, more symmetric faces, even—maybe—more animated faces.

So what was it about this one that kept pulling him in, as if he was nothing more than just some loose iron filing and she was this large, compelling and damn sexy magnet?

Move, damn it, Baker! Move! Get the hell out of here! Go!

And yet, he didn't.

What he did do was place his hands on either side of her shoulders, anchoring her in place ever so lightly. And then, in the next heartbeat, he found himself lowering his face to hers.

Lowering his lips to hers.

And then, just like that, there was no more lowering, no more mental skirmishes with small, annoying inner voices telling him to get the hell out of there before he got in over his head.

He was already in over his head.

He knew that from the first second his mouth touched hers.

But it didn't keep him from savoring the taste he'd discovered. Didn't keep him, for one insanely head-spinning second, from losing himself in her.

Chapter 10

Time stretched out as one second fed on another.

One taste begged for a second.

And then a third.

Cole's hands slipped from her shoulders and framed Nika's face. He gathered her to him as he deepened a kiss that was already far too deep for him to safely tread water.

He was swimming for his life.

And coming perilously close to going down for the third time.

Damn, he hadn't expected this. Hadn't expected something so insignificant as a mere kiss to open up a door that released something wild and raw within him. Never in a million years would he have said that someone as innocent looking as this woman could have elicited this sort of a reaction from him.

And yet, she was.

Big-time.

Oh God, this was it. This was what she had resigned herself to believe *didn't* exist in the world. She'd once prayed with every fiber of her being that something like this would find her, but as she grew older, Nika began to realize that things like this just didn't happen. That the feel of lightning striking in your veins was the stuff that movies and books and dreams were made out of, but as far as reality went, well, it just didn't happen. Reality promised to be a letdown, and she'd made her peace with that.

Until this moment, she'd been content to be the doctor, the daughter, the niece, the friend that she was to the various people in her life. What she hadn't been—and it had been all right with her until just this moment—was a woman. A woman with a woman's desires and needs. That part of her had somehow gotten buried, lost in the shuffle to be all those other things, and be them to the utmost of her ability. And consequently, she'd never been in love. Never made love.

But at this moment, all she wanted was to be a woman. To be with him.

To be a lover. *His* lover.

She wanted to follow this racing feeling that pulsated through her to its natural conclusion. *Ached* to follow it to its natural conclusion. She knew there'd be consequences, and ultimately, there'd be pain. Men like Cole Baker didn't stay put, didn't settle down.

But that was something she'd think about later. Right now, all that mattered was this untamed excitement she was feeling.

"Do you want to come inside for a minute?" she whispered against Cole's mouth.

The next moment, she felt that mouth form a single word.

"Yes."

Nika was still clutching the key to her apartment in her hand. Her heart pounding, she moved over only enough to be able to somehow insert the key into the lock and turn it. Grasping the doorknob, her mouth still very much sealed to Cole's, Nika managed to twist it and get the door open.

Holding on to her tightly, Cole moved into her apartment, bringing her with him.

And then Cole's cell phone began to ring.

The insistent sound shattered the moment into tiny little bits.

She heard Cole mutter an oath under his breath, draw away from her and yank the offending communication device out of his pocket. The second he put it to his ear, her cell began to ring, demanding her attention.

Nika's heart sank as a premonition told her it wasn't a coincidence. Still, she fervently hoped it was as she took her cell out of her purse.

Even as she did so, her eyes never left Cole's face, taking in every nuance. She almost felt his expression as it hardened. Whatever it was, it wasn't good.

Nika barely remembered mumbling, "Hello?" into her phone.

"Dr. Pulaski?" a husky, breathless voice asked. "It's Gerald."

An image of the imposing orderly flashed through her mind's eye. The man who'd helped Cole get her out of the elevator shaft. Why was Gerald calling her? And who had given him her number? "This is Dr. Pulaski. What's wrong, Gerald?"

"This wasn't my idea, Doctor," his voice was apologetic. "Shelley, the evening nurse, asked me to call you. It's Mr. Peters."

Her breath backed up in her chest. She stopped looking at Cole and turned away, creating a semblance of privacy for herself. The bad feeling she had turned to a worse one.

"What about him?" she asked, her voice deadly still as she hoped against hope that she wasn't going to hear what she was afraid of hearing.

The solemn voice on the other end said, "He died. His heart just gave out."

It didn't seem possible. There was no record of the man even having a heart condition, and nothing had shown up on any tests. Kidney stones were responsible for bringing him to the E.R. and those had successfully been broken up. He had the heart of a forty-year-old.

"But he was supposed to be leaving today," Nika protested, as if that could somehow change the outcome. "He was all right when I saw him. I signed him out."

She pressed her lips together, banking down the sudden wave of sadness that threatened to overwhelm her. She'd promised to stop by before leaving for the day to discuss her idea about finding him a housemate, but one of her other patients had suddenly had a seizure and had needed all of her attention. By the time he'd been stabilized, it was time for her to meet Cole.

Would she have been able to save the old man if she'd kept her promise to drop by his room before she left?

"Not anymore," Gerald told her quietly. "I wouldn't have bothered you, Doctor, but Nurse Shelley thought you'd want to know."

Yes, she wanted to know. "She was right, Gerald," Nika said numbly. "Thanks for calling."

Feeling as if she was drugged and sleepwalking, she pressed the button that ended the call and dropped her cell into her purse without looking.

"There's been another one," Cole told her grimly, closing his cell phone.

"I know." She struggled to bank down the lost feeling wafting through her.

What was going on? *Was* there someone deliberately killing old people? She'd been the one to call attention to this, but even so, it seemed so horribly improbable. Joshua Peters wouldn't have hurt a fly—why do away with him? "I just got a call from the hospital. Joshua Peters died."

He had another possible homicide on his hands. And in all likelihood, a serial killer. So why did he have this overwhelming urge to shut all that out and just get back to kissing her?

Cole forced himself to focus.

"I've got to go," he told her. It was not without regret. But he was a cop, and death came before life in this case.

She pulled her door closed and locked it. "I'm coming with you."

He wasn't about to bring her to what was now a crime scene. Even though she was no stranger to death, this was his territory, not hers. "Veronika, I can't—"

There was no way she was going to stay behind. "Mr. Peters was *my* patient," she insisted. "He was fine this afternoon when I saw him. Not happy about being released, but fine."

Her words stopped him in his tracks. "Why wasn't he happy about being released?" He had no idea if this meant anything or not, but at this point, he needed all the input he could gather together. Somewhere in all the unsorted information he'd collected about the late patients was the reason this was happening. He just had to make sense of it.

"Take me with you and I'll tell you," Nika bargained. She saw the hesitation in his eyes. She had him on the ropes and he was wavering, she thought. "If you don't take me, I'm still going to get there. It'll just take me longer by bus."

He knew she wasn't bluffing. She was as good as gone. "You are one stubborn woman."

"Never claimed not to be," she replied. She wasn't about to celebrate a victory yet. "That's one of my outstanding features. Stubbornness is in the genes," she told him.

He could believe it. Cole led the way back to the elevator. He repeated his question as they walked. "All right, tell me why Joshua Peters wasn't happy about being released?"

Oh no, it wasn't going to be that easy. "I'll tell you when I'm in your car and you're driving back toward the hospital."

He pressed for the elevator and then glared at her incredulously. "Don't trust me?"

"Ordinarily, I'd say yes, because that's just the way I am. Trusting." And, at times, that was a liability. She'd gotten hurt that way and definitely taken advantage of. But she refused to surrender her faith, her optimism. The day she did, the other side won. "But in this case," she told him, "no. You'd leave me and tell me it's for my own good. Meanwhile, you'd be hoping that I wouldn't make good on my promise of taking the bus."

The elevator arrived and Cole ushered her in before him, then pressed for the first floor and hoped they could get there without having to pick up any additional passengers.

"I know better," he answered. "There's no point in

trying to abandon you. You'd walk if you had to, but you'd get there."

She smiled as they rode down. "You are beginning to get to know me, aren't you?"

"Yes," he answered. "I am."

And heaven only knew if that was a good thing or a bad one, he added silently. He had the uneasy feeling that this little bit of a woman could very well be his undoing, taking him to places he had vehemently vowed never to frequent again.

"Okay, now tell me," Cole all but ordered as he drove out of the parking structure and onto the street again. Twilight was darkening the streets, ushering in a velvety night. His headlights illuminated the path before them a few feet at a time. It wasn't foggy, but it definitely was unclear.

"He hated living in the nursing home, said his kids sold his house out from under him and took some of the money to set him up at the nursing home. He complained to me more than once that he hated living with old people because they were all obsessed with issuing periodic proclamations about their bodily functions. That and, according to him, they smelled of death."

Not exactly a selling feature, he thought. "Peters said that?"

"More or less," Nika answered. When he looked at her, waiting, she added, "I dressed it up a little, but I'm not exaggerating the way he felt about living in that nursing home. I told him that I would try to help him get his own place and share expenses with a housemate. I know several people who lived with elderly citizens, helping them out in exchange for a break in the rent. I also have had contact with some people who really want to get out of living in nursing homes, but they can't afford their own place. I was sure that one of them would be open to this arrangement," she said with a sad smile. "I wanted to help him regain his sense of freedom and dignity."

Frustrated, angry, Nika blew out a breath and stared through the window at the world that was now enshrouded in darkness.

"And now he's gone." She snapped her fingers. "Just like that."

Cole listened to her as his mind pulled in connections, searching for any kind of red flag, any kind of clue to send him off in a new direction.

"Who called you just now?" he asked as he eased his car around a corner.

"Gerald." She glanced at Cole. "I think his last name is Mayfield. He's an orderly on the floor tonight. Oh," she recalled again, "he's the one who helped you get me out of the elevator shaft."

"He has your phone number?" Cole questioned. Was she friendly with the orderly? Or was there something more? And why did that seem to matter to him beyond just applying it to the case? If she was involved with the orderly, then she was lying about not being sure of the man's last name, and Cole's gut told him she didn't lie. Even so, he pressed, "Isn't that a little unusual?"

"It would be if he had my number, but he doesn't. At least, I never gave it to him. That's not to say it's not available through the hospital intranet." She mentally pushed the sadness she felt to one side and tried to think. "Gerald said that one of the nurses, Shelley Wallace," she said, guessing his next question, "asked him to call me. Most likely, she got my cell number for him. I think they all know how attached I get to the patients in the unit." She pressed her lips together, talking more to herself than to him. "I shouldn't, but I do."

Cole's voice was stony. "Attachments are how people get hurt."

His tone had her looking at him. She wanted to ask the detective if he was speaking from personal experience, but something warned her away from the subject. Right now, there were a lot of emotions dancing between them and not all of them had to do with the man they were going to the hospital to view one last time.

"Maybe I should move my grandmother," he said, breaking the painful silence that was pulsating and growing between them.

"Move her?" Nika echoed in surprise. "Move her to where?"

"To another hospital." He didn't want to get so involved in this case that he overlooked the very obvious: that quite possibly his grandmother was in danger. "There's obviously something going on at Patience Memorial and—"

She didn't let him finish. "Don't do anything rash," Nika begged. "Dr. Goodfellow is an excellent surgeon and so's Dr. Chase, the surgeon who's scheduled to do her breast biopsy once her blood pressure is within the acceptable parameters."

"That won't do her any good if something happens to her before she can have the procedures done," Cole pointed out.

Nika shifted in her seat. "Listen to me. Going to a good hospital and lining up the best surgeons is more important than a lot of people realize. Not every surgeon is worth the title and, as for the hospital, you want one that polices its own staff to make sure that mistakes are kept at a minimum. This hospital has an incredible track record for excellence. That's not as easy to come by as it sounds."

Still, he had his doubts. "Doesn't do much good when there's some kind of maniac running loose, eliminating old people at will."

"Maybe it's not at will," Nika countered, reviewing the list she'd given him in her mind. "Maybe whoever's doing this isn't doing it just willy-nilly or for the money. Maybe—"

"Willy-nilly," he repeated, sparing her a look that bordered on amusement. "Who says 'willy-nilly' these days?"

She frowned. Phraseology was not the point here. "Sorry, I've been too busy going to medical school to update my vocabulary," she replied. "The point is I don't think you should move your grandmother. I can talk to my uncle to see if he can somehow subtly up the security detail in the hospital. He knows the head of security here, and Uncle Josef can make sure that there's someone watching out for your grandmother at all times," she said.

She saw Cole's hands tighten ever so slightly on the wheel. "I can watch out for my own grandmother."

She knew all about pride. She'd lived with it most of her life. Her mother reeked of it. But there was a time when pride had to take a backseat to logic.

"Cole, you're working a case. Solving that case will keep your grandmother safe. But meanwhile, you can't work the case and be with your grandmother at the same time—unless you have some kind of secret ability you haven't told me about."

He had lots of secrets he hadn't told her about, Cole

thought. She hadn't a clue how dark his soul really was. But the ability to be two places at once was not among his secrets.

When he made no comment about her argument, Nika pushed a little harder. "Cole, you have to let other people help if they can. Nobody's an island."

He was, he thought. But at the same moment, he thought of how he would feel if something happened to his grandmother. He was vulnerable when it came to the old woman's well-being. That didn't make him much of an island.

And then there was the matter of the woman in the passenger seat. Another possible breach in his walls. He'd almost made a grave mistake earlier. The call from the patrolman who'd been summoned to the hospital had wound up inadvertently saving him. He was going to have to get a tighter rein on himself. A tighter rein on emotions that threatened to break free.

"If you say so," he muttered.

"I say so," Nika responded with feeling.

Her heart ached for him and she couldn't even put into words why.

Arriving at the hospital, Nika lost no time hurrying to the Geriatrics Unit. Her heart pounded all the way there.

Mr. Peters was still in his room. When she walked in, at first glance, the old man looked as if he was just sleeping. But Death had a way of removing a victim's personality, of making their features sink in just enough to announce that he had been by, and had taken their soul.

Moved, Nika took the old man's cold hand in hers, lacing her fingers through digits that were growing stiff.

Rigor was setting in, she noted, which meant that he hadn't been dead all that long.

Could she have prevented it? If she'd come by, instead of making a note to get back to him when she could, would he be alive this moment?

"Oh, Mr. Peters, I am so very sorry," she whispered to the man who could no longer hear. "Sorry I didn't get you out of here when I talked to you today."

Her mind continued to torture her. Had he died in that window of time when she should have been here, but was in the operating room instead? Right now, she didn't know. All she knew was that she ached and felt horribly guilty.

As if reading her thoughts, Cole stepped closer to her until he was all but her shadow. "It's not your fault," he told her firmly.

"If I'd stayed, if I'd been in the room with him, whoever it was who did this wouldn't have been able to get to him."

"Maybe," he agreed. "And maybe whoever's doing this would have waited for you to leave and then come in to end Mr. Peters's life." An idea came to him. "Was he suffering?"

"Mr. Peters? Outside of regular aches and pains, I'd say that he was suffering emotionally more than physically."

She'd piqued his interest. "How so?"

"He didn't want to go back to the nursing home," she repeated. "It made him feel as if he was useless, that he'd been thrown away by his family and society in general." Maybe she'd call her mother tonight, Nika thought. Just to touch base and let the woman know that she was loved.

Nika looked around the man's bed to double-check.

There were no IV drips. There never had been in his case. So death had to have been delivered to him via another method.

Very gently, as if he could still feel her fingers, she spread the lids of one of his eyes apart just enough to examine the white region. There was no redness, no sign of broken blood vessels, which would have indicated that he'd been smothered or deprived of oxygen in some other fashion.

"What are you doing?" Cole asked as she straightened up again and began to perform a quick examination of the victim's skin.

"Looking for marks."

She didn't have to look long. There was a small, almost imperceptible hole in the old man's right inner thigh. It was located directly at the site of a major artery.

It was, she concluded, that exact site that Death had entered and found Joshua Peters.

Chapter 11

"What's all the commotion out there?" Ericka Baker asked the moment Nika and Cole walked into her room.

Since she was here, Nika had decided to look in on the woman right after she'd signed off on Joshua Peters. She was afraid that Cole's grandmother might have heard about the latest death and grown apprehensive. Stress wasn't going to help lower the woman's blood pressure.

Ericka's question made it obvious that no one had told the elderly woman anything.

"Just someone checking out of the hospital," Nika replied evasively. Her eyes met Cole's. She saw the all but imperceptible nod. He approved of her vague answer.

Ericka frowned. Her eyes darted suspiciously from her doctor to her grandson. "At this hour?"

"It just worked out that way," Cole told her, relieved that the curtain to her room had been drawn all this time.

"Wish someone would take me home," Ericka grumbled. Her frown deepened as she looked expectantly at her grandson. "The food's terrible here and the service—" She sighed deeply before continuing. "Sometimes I have to wait five, maybe ten minutes before anyone shows up when I press that damn buzzer." She nodded at the nurse's call button.

Nika smiled at her. The nurses prided themselves on their quick response time at Patience Memorial. "That's not waiting, that's a blink of an eye."

"Easy for you to say." Ericka waved a blue-veined hand at her. "You've got time. For all I know, all I've got left is 'a blink of an eye.'"

Nika patted Ericka's bony shoulder lightly. "You're going to live to see your great-grandchildren."

Ericka's eyes shifted over toward her grandson. "Not if I have to wait for him to make a move." And then, just like that, the woman's eyes lit up. It was like watching the birth of an idea, Nika thought. Ericka's eyes shifted back to her. "Didn't you say that you weren't with anyone?"

A person with the IQ of a shoelace could see where this was going, but Nika played along. "Yes, I did."

"How about my grandson?" Ericka propositioned boldly.

"G." Cole didn't raise his voice, but the warning note was nonetheless evident in his voice.

Ericka waved her hand at him, dismissing his unspoken protest. She continued staring at Nika pointedly. "Do you think he's good-looking?" she asked.

Paraphrasing a line out of *The Wizard of Oz*, a movie both he and his late brother had watched countless times during their brief childhood, Cole intoned, "Pay no attention to the woman in the bed."

He was doing a masterful job hiding his embarrassment, but Nika could sense it and couldn't help being just the slightest bit amused by his dilemma. She'd been on the receiving end of this kind of a scene more than once, listening to her mother despair about her ever getting married. She liked seeing this human side to Cole and she knew *exactly* how he had to be feeling.

"Yes," she replied, managing to keep a straight face, "I think he's good-looking."

Cole's grandmother nodded, pleased. It was obvious to Nika that she had just passed some kind of test and progressed to the next level.

"You're a not-bad-looking young woman," Ericka continued. Her thin lips pulled back into a knowing smile. "You two would make very pretty babies."

Okay, he'd been the dutiful grandson long enough. He was drawing the line before G offered the doctor five horses and a mule to take him off her hands.

"That's enough, G," he told her sternly.

"Well, you would," Ericka protested, annoyed at the interruption. "And at my age, I deserve to see my greatgrandchild before I kick the bucket. You're not getting any younger, either, you know, Coleman," she declared tersely.

Time to cut this short, Nika thought. "There'll be no buckets kicked on my watch, young lady," Nika informed Cole's grandmother, then changed the subject. "I think that your blood pressure will be down sufficiently enough for Dr. Chase to operate on you in the next couple of days, and we can get back to addressing the reason why you're here in the first place." Finished, Nika offered the woman an encouraging smile.

"Yeah, to make you and the other doctors all fat and rich," Ericka grumbled.

Cole looked at Nika and she could have sworn she saw an apology in his eyes. He came closer to his grandmother's bed.

"G, were you always this sunny and happy and I just didn't notice, or is this behavior something new?" he asked the woman.

"You try lying around in a hospital all day and see if you wind up being all smiles and happiness by the end of the day. Day? Hell, boy, you wouldn't last until noon," she pronounced with a quick, firm bob of her head.

"No," he agreed. He'd never done waiting well. It was a given. "You're right, I wouldn't. You're definitely a better man than I am, G."

Ericka raised her chin, proud to have won that round. "And don't you forget it," she retorted, crossing her arms before her as if to seal the argument. "What are you doing here anyway?" she asked. Her eyes narrowed into suspicious slits. "Did she call you and tell you to come? Am I dying?" she demanded. Throwing back her shoulders like a young recruit, she told him, "If I'm dying, I have a right to know."

Nika placed a calming hand on the woman's wrist, drawing Ericka's attention back to her. "Do you feel like you're dying?"

The question took some of the wind out of Ericka's sails. "No."

"Then you're not dying," Nika assured her. "You'd be the first to know if you were. You know your body a lot better than anyone else does."

Ericka blew out a breath, clearly annoyed. "They pay you for that kind of advice?"

"Yes," Nika deadpanned.

"Do they pay you well?" Ericka pressed, her sharp, hawklike eyes pinning her down.

Nika smiled. "No, not really." She was earning a mere forty thousand a year for working herself to the bone on twenty minutes sleep a night. At least, it felt as if she was only getting twenty minutes' sleep. Maybe it was thirty-five.

The answer pleased Ericka and she nodded her head. "I can understand why."

"Be nice, G," Cole instructed.

Her head snapped around in order for her to look at him. "This *is* nice."

"Right," he agreed fondly. "I forgot."

Nika and Cole remained in his grandmother's room for another fifteen minutes. Though she struggled to remain awake, Ericka lost that battle and dropped off to sleep. The moment she did, they slipped out of her room like two teenagers bent on breaking curfew without getting caught.

When they were in the hallway, Cole struggled for a moment, searching for the words, before he apologized. "I'm sorry about my grandmother."

The apology surprised her. If asked, Nika would have said that the man didn't know how to apologize. She found that she liked these softer traits that she was being allowed to glimpse. It meant that the man had more than looks and brains going for him. She found his affection for his grandmother incredibly appealing.

As if he wasn't already.

"Don't be," Nika told him. "I've put up with a lot

worse, trust me. Your grandmother's kind of cute in her own unique way." She was aware of Cole looking at her. More than looking, he seemed to be *studying* her. Her skin began to tingle. This was becoming a habit. "What?"

He shook his head, shoving his hands into his pockets. "Nothing. Just trying to see if your nose was going to grow, that's all."

He didn't believe her, she thought, amused.

"I really have connected with worse," she assured him. "Your grandmother's just frustrated. I can't say I blame her. Most people hate being confined and restricted. She's a feisty lady who likes calling her own shots. She can't do that in the hospital. She feels as if she's at the mercy of whoever's on duty. That kind of thing makes her curt and abrupt."

"And you *like* dealing with people like that?"

Nika never hesitated. "Yes."

That didn't make any sense to him. He wasn't a people person to begin with, but if he were, all things being equal, these wouldn't be the kind of people he would have chosen to be around. "Why?"

"For the most part, these people have worked all their lives, given of themselves and asked for little or nothing in return beyond a paycheck. That kind of sacrifice earns them the right to be treated with dignity and respect. They deserve to feel that their opinions still count, that they can have some kind of say when it comes to managing their own lives."

Her smile broadened. "And, like I said, I like hearing stories and they like telling them. That makes it a win-win relationship."

Not in his opinion, but it was obviously enough for

her. There was a great deal more to this woman than met the eye at first. "Whatever you say."

They weren't all that different, she thought. "You feel a little like I do."

"How do you figure that?"

"Because you worry about your grandmother," she said simply. When he stared at her, a slight furrow forming between his eyes, she explained her reasoning. "You're here for her, instead of just shrugging off the responsibility. You could easily just hide behind your work and tell her that you're too busy to come by. But you don't, because you care."

There was a reason for that. "I *owe* her," he emphasized.

Maybe that was the key to making him understand her position. "And maybe I feel like I'm taking the place of people who owe these people something."

Cole laughed shortly and shook his head. "I won't even pretend that I understand what you just said." And then he nodded toward the elevator. "You ready to go home?"

She was more than ready at this point. "Yes." She assumed from his question that he intended to take her to her apartment. "But don't you have to go down to the precinct?"

"I can drop you off on the way," he told her. "Besides, there's not all that much I can do about Mr. Peters's less than timely demise tonight. The crime scene unit has to process his room first. If I go to the precinct, all I'm going to wind up doing is staring at a bulletin board, trying to make sense out of all these pieces that still haven't come together."

She felt tired, but oddly restless at the same time. "I could help you," she volunteered.

He laughed, shaking his head. "I can't bring you down to the station. Captain doesn't like civilians wandering around his squad room."

"I wouldn't be wandering, I'd be staring at the same bulletin board you were. Helping," she repeated.

"I appreciate the offer," he told her. He still wasn't going to bring her to the precinct. "How about we compromise and you can give me your thoughts while I drive you back to your apartment?"

Did he think she was too tired to understand what he was doing? "That's not a compromise, that's you getting your way."

Taking her arm, Cole moved Nika along a little faster toward the elevator. "I was hoping you wouldn't notice."

Laughing, she said, "You have to work on learning to be more subtle."

"I'll put it on my 'to-do' list." He was also going to have to learn, Cole added silently, not to react to the sound of her laugh, which seemed to wrap itself around him like a warm embrace on a cold winter's morning.

Though she knew that it was unreasonable, because Cole had a boatload of work waiting for him no matter what he said, Nika found herself hoping that he would bring her up to her door again.

And hoping for more than that.

She quietly held her breath as they drew near her apartment building. This time, she kept the suggestion that was on the tip of her tongue to herself, waiting to see what Cole was going to do. Waiting to see if he would just pull up to the building's entrance and merely let her out, or if he would drive his car into the parking structure the way he had last time.

He passed the entrance and entered the parking garage.

Nika held her breath until he parked his car.

"I'd like to come up," he told her quietly once he turned off the ignition. She realized that it was more a question than a statement. He was actually asking her if that was what she wanted as well.

Nika made her choice—as if she could say anything else. "I'd like that."

Damn, what was he doing? Cole silently demanded, bewildered. Why was he putting himself into this kind of a position? It was like someone with a glass jaw leading with his chin in a boxing match. He was asking for trouble, for complications, for things he had no time for and didn't want. Complications that inevitably aroused feelings.

And yet...

And yet, there was something about her, something that made him feel alive, that connected him to a world he'd long since walked away from.

He'd forgotten he could actually *feel* anything.

He'd voluntarily been on the outside for so long, he'd come to believe that was where he belonged. Being on the outside suited him. Allowed him to do his job with no interference. Until this latest development with his grandmother, he had just touched base with the woman on occasion, remembering her on days the greeting card companies declared were important. But beyond that, he lived and breathed in a rarified zone that allowed his heart to function, to beat and direct blood to all his vital organs. But feel? His heart wasn't capable of doing that.

At least, it couldn't before.

Now he wasn't so sure.

And a large part of him resisted things changing, resisted finding out that his heart could do anything beyond beat.

But the temptation of Nika's mouth drove his resolutions out of his head, propelling them into a zone that was packed away out of the light of day, a darkened no-man's-land.

The hallways of her apartment building were carpeted, yet Cole could almost hear his own footsteps as he came closer and closer to his undoing, all the while guiding her to her door.

"I'd better go," he heard himself saying as she took out her key.

No, please don't go. To come so close only to still be so far away isn't fair. Nika raised her eyes to his. "Ever have a feeling of déjà vu?"

He was having it right now. "Sometimes," Cole allowed.

She was on her toes, her mouth suddenly closer than his resolve. "I'm having that feeling now," she told him, her voice a whisper, her breath a temptation.

Self-preservation was a very finely honed instinct for a cop. His instincts told him that this was where he was supposed to turn around and walk away. It was called survival.

Nowhere in the self-preservation bylaws did it say anything about his diving out of an airplane headfirst without a parachute strapped on.

But that was exactly what he wound up doing when he pulled her into his arms and kissed her. Not gently or slowly or with any sort of sense of exploration, the way he had last time. He kissed her hard, as if he was fully prepared to stick his arm into the fire and deal with all the consequences that were coming.

He'd never been so unprepared in his life.

Cole swiftly saw that he had no control in this situation. There wasn't a single shot he could call. Instead, there was this wild sense of abandonment washing over him. Not as in being abandoned, but in throwing his soul to the winds. All he wanted was to feel that wild rush in his veins that kissing her inexplicably unleashed. Nothing else mattered.

His head began to spin at an incredibly fast speed, promising more of the same.

Cole wasn't sure just how they managed to get into her apartment. Didn't know if she'd unlocked the door before this wild ride began, or if she'd practiced some kind of sleight of hand and unlocked the door while lost in the throes of this kiss, but suddenly, they were no longer outside but in.

The door closing registered in some faraway region of his brain that was still capable of collecting data. But just barely so. The preponderance of his brain was busy being enticed. Busy savoring the mounting passion that gave no sign of abating.

Ever.

Uncustomarily eager, Cole began undressing her and wound up all but ripping Nika's clothes from her body as he struggled hard to contain his all but overpowering excitement.

He thought he heard something ripping and then realized that it was his own clothes that had sustained the damage. She was tugging and inadvertently tearing his clothes from him, whether intentionally or by accident didn't matter. What mattered was that it was happening.

* * *

It was hard to think when her brain was wrapped in a fiery haze. Heaven help her, she'd never, ever felt this way and it wasn't just because she'd never been with a man this way before. It was because she'd never felt the desire to be with a man this intensely. No one had ever lit a fire beneath her even remotely close to the way this man had, never made her want things the way Cole did, just by existing, by breathing and being near her.

She was a doctor and knew all about the logistics, the mechanics of how a man and woman came together, but what she had no knowledge of was that elusive, missing X-factor. No prior knowledge of that wildness that ran through the blood and ultimately led to this fascinating place where passion reigned supreme and nothing else mattered except achieving the ultimate connection, the ultimate bonding with the man her soul was calling out to.

Until the fateful day she'd gotten stuck in that elevator, she'd envied her sister and her cousins and her friends because that head-over-heels sensation had come into their lives but never once into hers.

And now it had, taking her prisoner.

Nikka thought that their coming together would be quick. That Cole would enter her and that the union would be sealed.

She hadn't expected him to go out of his way to pleasure her. To heat a body that was already burning for him.

When she felt his mouth gliding along her skin, felt him lightly skim his lips along quivering sections of her body, she all but exploded as she desperately tried to hold off experiencing what she assumed was saved for the last moment.

But thirty years without any release made for a great deal of pressure building up and his mouth and hands were too clever at eliciting responses from her. Suddenly, just like that, she found herself on the receiving end of a climax. And then, to her astonishment, one climax flowered into another as he brought his lips to the side of her throat, to her belly, to her breasts, effectively reducing her to a cauldron of throbbing needs and wants.

Making her climax, only to have her renew the climb again.

She hadn't realized that there was actual magic involved until she'd experienced it.

Hardly able to draw in a breath, Nika tightened her fingertips on his shoulders as she felt him enter her.

Her eyes were shut tight when she felt him hesitate. Instinctively knowing what he had to be thinking, Nika immediately raised her hips and her mouth at the same time, sealing her lips to his as she urged him on with her body.

Unable to resist, to do what he knew he should, Cole didn't stop. He pushed in. He felt her quick intake of breath less than half a second before she began the dance that was theirs alone. The dance he unconsciously knew he would remember for the rest of his life.

He stopped processing sensations and just lost himself in her.

Chapter 12

The moment the euphoria that lovemaking had generated began to recede, guilt descended on Cole with the force of an anvil that had been dropped from the roof of a five-story building. He didn't know what to say, or how to begin to apologize.

Didn't know how to take back that which couldn't be taken back.

Every apology began with a first word. He forced one out, not really knowing what was going to follow in its wake.

"Why?"

Nika knew what was coming. Saw it in his eyes and didn't want the question, the assumption he was making, to be anywhere near the fireworks still settling down within her. She wanted to be able to savor what had happened between them for just a little longer.

But that wasn't possible anymore.

She put her fingers to his lips to still them and shut away the words that Cole was so obviously struggling with.

"Because," she answered, saying the universal word that had been known to quiet arguments across the board and was the tacitly understood explanation for everything, large or small, that required a myriad of words to put it to rest. Parents used it all the time when they were at a loss for exact explanations.

Because.

Cole gently took her hand away from his mouth, his eyes giving voice to the confusion and the guilt that were still square-dancing within him. He was having a great deal of trouble understanding what he'd just learned to be true.

"You never…?"

Nika merely smiled in response, preferring to move ahead. "I have now."

"But not before?" he asked incredulously, still unable to finish his sentence out loud. How could a woman, especially a beautiful woman, come to this point in her life and still be a virgin? It just didn't seem possible.

And yet, it was obviously true in this case.

"No," she replied simply, wishing he would drop the subject and allow her to just bow away from it gracefully, to glory in this new threshold she'd crossed. She didn't want to go into explanations.

But avoiding them would have been too easy, and she'd known from the moment she'd laid eyes on him that Detective Cole Baker was not an easy man. Not by any stretch of the imagination. Why should making love with him be any different?

"How is that possible?" he asked. What, had she been raised in some tower, like Rapunzel?

"No one's given you the birds-and-bees talk?" she asked, the corners of her mouth curving, seeking refuge in humor for a moment. "I have this wonderful book I could recommend—"

He cut her short. This wasn't a joke. Not to him. Her situation and what he'd done brought a vast responsibility in its wake.

"You know what I mean." He struggled not to snap out the words. It wasn't Veronika he was angry with, it was himself. "How do you get to be your age and not...?"

His voice trailed off again as he looked at her, completely stunned, completely floored as well as speechless.

"Choice," Nika told him. Then, because she saw that the single word wasn't enough, she added, "Because I didn't feel that making love with someone was something you just did at the end of a date. I wanted someone I respected and admired to be the first man I slept with. And, just as importantly, I wanted the first man to be someone who could make the earth move for me just by his proximity. I kept hoping someone would come along who met those requirements. I wasn't about to settle for anything less."

The implied compliment stunned him. "And I meet those requirements for you?" he asked in disbelief.

She lifted one shoulder in a quick shrug, a silent tribute to the whimsy of a fate that saw fit to bring together unlikely duos, and throw into the mix electricity, like the kind she'd felt with him the first time her body had slid against his.

"Like it or not," she acknowledged, "you do."

"That first part, 'like it or not,'" he repeated, "are you referring to your reaction to the situation, or what you assume is *my* reaction to it?"

Okay, the man had just lost her. "Excuse me?"

Cole tried to rephrase his question. "Are you saying that you aren't too happy about the turn of events, or that you're thinking that perhaps I'm not happy about what just happened between us?"

Before answering, Nika took in a long breath and pulled down a multicolored throw she had slung over the back of the sofa. She wrapped it around herself like a woolly toga. She was suddenly feeling extremely exposed.

"I'm saying that you're really overthinking things," she told him glibly. "I'm also saying I have no regrets."

"You might want to rethink that," he warned her. "I'm not exactly a happy-go-lucky person."

It was hard not to laugh and impossible not to grin. "I hadn't noticed."

She needed to know, he thought. To know how dark his soul was. The only way to tell her was straight out, no embellishments. She deserved that. So he began.

"My father was a soldier," he said without preamble. "He was killed his second day overseas by a bomb that was strapped to a nine-year-old kid. Six months later, my younger brother, Steve, was knocked off his bicycle by a hit-and-run driver. The guy never even stopped. Steve died on the way to the hospital. Losing Steve was the final straw for my mother. It broke her and she never really came around. One day, not too long after that, I came home from school and she called me into the kitchen. When I walked in, she shot me, then turned the gun on herself. She died instantly." Looking away, he struggled to keep the memory at arm's length. "I guess she didn't want to leave me behind.

"They tell me it was touch-and-go for me for a while. When I finally woke up, I was in the hospital and G was sitting there beside my bed. She looked drawn, like she hadn't slept in days. The first thing she said to me was, 'About time you pulled through.'" A fond smile touched his lips. "I owe her a lot."

Nika felt her heart twisting in her chest. "Oh God, Cole, I don't know what to say."

"Don't say anything." He hadn't told her because he wanted sympathy. "I just wanted you to know who you're getting mixed up with."

"I already know that." Her eyes held his. "You're a survivor."

"Yeah, well, surviving seems to be the thing to do." He looked at her now. She wasn't getting up. She was still here. He didn't know if that was good or bad—for either of them. "About those regrets—"

Was he going to tell her that he regretted what happened between them after all? "Still don't have them," she told him. "If you do, I'm sorry, but I'm afraid there will be no refunds issued."

His eyebrows drew together in a confused V. "What?"

She shrugged uncomfortably, dismissing her last words. "Feeble joke," she admitted. "Sorry."

Getting up off the sofa, she bent down to quickly retrieve her clothes. Holding them against her, she began heading toward the next room, toward the first private area where she could get dressed.

She nearly made it all the way out of the room before his words stopped her.

"I don't regret making love with you," Cole said, his voice low as he addressed his words to her back. "I just regret not knowing you were a virgin."

Nika slowly turned around. "And if you'd known, then what? You wouldn't have bothered?" What else could he mean by saying he'd wished he'd known? The man was obviously accustomed to experienced women, not one who behaved as if she'd just been transported to an incredible alternate universe.

"The word 'bothered' doesn't belong in this sentence," he informed her. "If I'd known that this was your first time, I would have tried to make it special," he explained tersely.

"Make it special," she echoed. It was her turn to be confused. "As opposed to what? Fantastic? Because that was what it was. Fantastic. Any more 'special' than that and I might not have survived the experience."

"Fantastic?" he repeated.

She couldn't read his expression in order to gauge his feelings. The man was probably a world-class poker player. Nika nodded. "That was the word."

He was having trouble processing this. "You thought what we did was fantastic?"

The smile began in her eyes, filtering through to all parts of her. "Absolutely."

Cole got up. Since she had taken the throw for herself, there was nothing for him to wrap around himself. Consequently, he crossed to her as naked as he'd been while they'd made love. Nika felt her blood heating instantly, even as she struggled to keep her eyes on his face.

She wasn't entirely successful in her efforts.

"Any way I can talk you out of getting dressed?" he asked, taking her into his arms.

Nika let the throw slip away from her body and fall to the floor like a deep sigh. The bunched-up clothes joined it.

"You just did," she told him, just before she sealed her lips to his.

This wasn't going well.

Twelve victims.

Twelve *alleged* victims, he silently corrected himself, had died in the Geriatrics Unit in the last eighteen months. Of those twelve, seven had had families, five hadn't. The families, other than the one couple who'd recently requested an autopsy and seemed far more interested in the financial rewards of an out-of-court settlement in exchange for keeping the allegation out of the public eye, were opposed to exhuming their loved ones.

No exhumation, no evidence that murder, rather than natural causes, was responsible for the victims' deaths.

He still had the late police sergeant, thanks to Nika's uncle. And, of course, there was that last man who'd died just before he was to be released and sent back to the nursing home. That made three, he reminded himself. Three dead people who'd met their end the same way. An air bubble had been injected into a major artery, causing them to convulse and die. Approximating a heart attack.

Cole thought that taking these deaths and extrapolating the evidence to hypothesize that the others had met the same ending was just a natural progression. The defense attorney, however, might just see it as a huge coincidence and petition to have the matter thrown out of court. Especially if Cole didn't come up with more evidence.

With two patients dying just in the last week, the pace was definitely picking up. He knew he was fighting the clock. He needed to find the killer before he—or she—struck again.

But right now he had no idea who to point a finger at. He had no viable suspects. And nothing to go on. Not without some kind of theory as to why these particular people had been picked and not any of the others.

Was this all the work of some maniac slipping into the hospital in order to take revenge for an imagined wrong that had been done to him or her? What kind of wrong? To whom? To the killer or someone he cared about?

Or was it someone on the staff doing away with these people?

That, he had to admit, was the more likely scenario, but if so, then who was it? And equally as important, *why* was he or she doing it? And what determined who the next victim was going to be?

Other than advanced age and being patients here on the fourth floor, the dead people had nothing uniformly in common. They weren't all women or all men, weren't from the same walk of life. Some were well off, others were poor. Some lived in nursing homes, some still lived in their own homes. Some were terminal, others weren't.

So what *was* it that connected them, other than Patience Memorial?

Cole stared at the overloaded bulletin board on the wall some ten feet away.

He rubbed his hand across his forehead, willing a headache away.

He couldn't come up with it, couldn't come up with

the key, the cipher, that would suddenly open up this case for him and get him moving in the right direction.

He was frustrated as hell.

Cole rocked back in his antiquated chair. It emitted a pathetic squeak every time he leaned all the way back in it. Now was no exception. It set his teeth on edge. Almost as much as the case was doing.

"Didn't anyone ever tell you not to rock back in your chair like that unless you want to wind up landing on your head?"

Cole swung around toward the speaker, belatedly banking down the instant rays of warmth that burst through the unguarded moment at the sound of the soft voice.

Nika's voice.

He half rose in his chair. When Nika dropped into the chair next to his desk, he sat back down again. "What are you doing here?"

"I have the day off," she reminded him. She'd mentioned that to him this morning before he'd left her bed to go to work. Amazingly enough, since that first night, there'd been a reason for them to get together every evening after that, including last night.

It went without saying that she'd gone to the hospital anyway, even though she was free to do whatever she wanted. What she'd wanted was to catch up on a few things at the hospital and to look in on her patients. To assure herself that they were still alive, still breathing.

Her uncle and a couple of his handpicked men were patrolling the floor as well as planted in prominent spots to demonstrate a show of solidarity to the mysterious killer so that, hopefully, there wouldn't be another casualty.

But she still worried. She couldn't help it. It was a congenital thing, handed down from her mother, who had made worry an art form.

"Anyway," Nika continued, "I came by to give you some good news."

He could certainly use that. Cole sat up, alert. "Someone caught the killer?"

"A different kind of good news," Nika amended, realizing her mistake. "You grandmother's blood pressure has finally gone down sufficiently enough for Dr. Chase to do the biopsy. His office assistant scheduled it for first thing tomorrow morning."

She was right. It *was* good news. But that also meant that the end results could bring bad news with it. If the mass wasn't benign...

"What time is 'first thing'?" he asked.

Chase's office assistant had booked the O.R. for the first slot of the day. "Seven-thirty in the morning."

He could be there before G was taken into the operating room. He knew she'd welcome the support, even if she wouldn't say it.

"You assisting?" he asked.

Nika nodded. "Already promised your grandmother I would be." She smiled, hoping to convey confidence to him so that he would feel more at ease about the surgery. "Can't go back on my word."

He knew she couldn't, no matter how casually she tendered that word. She was that kind of a woman, that kind of a person. Bound by her word. Honorable. Dedicated. A straight arrow the likes of which he wouldn't have believed actually existed if he hadn't met her.

If he hadn't watched her interact with his grandmother.

Cole laughed shortly, but the smile he offered to her was soft, kind. "I thought people like you went the way of the unicorn."

The look she gave him transformed her into innocence personified. "That's presupposing that unicorns don't exist."

He should have known that would be what she'd say. "Now you're going to tell me they actually *do* exist? Have you ever seen one?" he challenged.

"Just because you haven't seen one doesn't mean they don't exist," she pointed out.

"Makes a pretty good argument to me," he told her.

"I've never seen a native Samoan," she countered. "Doesn't mean they don't exist."

He laughed, shaking his head. "That's different, Veronika."

Her eyes were wide as she asked, "How?"

She didn't surrender easily, he'd give her that. "Plenty of *other* people have seen Samoans," he pointed out.

Nika inclined her head, as if indulging him. "Or so they say."

He laughed again, shaking his head. Amused. That was happening more often these days than he could remember it *ever* happening in years. She made him smile. "Is that the argument you use to prove that Santa Claus exists?"

"Who says he doesn't?" she asked innocently.

Cole raised his hands in the universal sign of surrender. "I yield," he declared. "You could get Satan to install air-conditioning in hell."

It was her turn to laugh. And to appreciate how comfortable they'd become with one another in such an incredibly short amount of time. She wished she could take it as a sign of things to come, but there was a part of her that was her mother's daughter. And her mother always expected the worst to happen.

"Now, there's a worthy project," she commented. "Too bad I'm too busy at the moment to tackle it."

Damn it, here he was, the middle of the day and he found himself wanting her. Wanting her even more now than he had the first time. Or the second. It seemed that each time he made love with her just stoked the fire rather than diminished it.

The woman was clearly a witch, there was no other explanation, he thought.

"Speaking of busy—" he began.

Nika looked up into his eyes, all but paralyzing his breath in his lungs. "Yes?"

"Are you?" he asked. Then added the word "busy" in case she wasn't following him.

Nika tossed her head, not quite able to carry off blasé, but then, she wasn't really trying to. "Depends on whether or not I get a good offer."

"Take-out, a movie rental and me," he rattled off, watching her face. "That good enough?"

She pretended to think it over for a moment. "Well, since that's the best I can do on short notice, I guess that's good enough," she told him, doing her best to maintain a straight face. But the sparkle in her eyes gave her away. "What time do you get off?"

"Barring any new bodies," which he fervently hoped there wouldn't be, "six o'clock."

The same time she usually did—if she were working today. "Why don't you swing by the hospital to see your grandmother," Nika suggested, "and then we'll take it from there?"

He'd always admired an organized mind. "You do think of everything, don't you?"

"Hey, multitasking is my middle name." Rising, she crossed to the bulletin board. Studying the various pieces of information, she looked at the charts. A small frown formed and played on her lips.

Cole got up and made his way over to her and the bulletin board. Her body language told him she thought she was onto something. It occurred to him that he was far more in tune to her than he was happy about. But that was a problem to be tackled another day. Right now, his chief priority was to catch the son of a bitch who was killing senior citizens.

"You see something?" he asked her.

It was a thought that had suddenly occurred to her, not something she'd seen on the bulletin board. "What if there isn't just one uniform thing?" she theorized, then whirled around to look at him, eager to get his input. "What if there're two?"

Was she talking about two theories? Or even more? "What do you mean?"

She was tripping over her own tongue, she thought, mentally chastizing herself. She needed to slow down. "What if the victims fall into two separate categories? The terminally sick ones and the ones who lived in nursing homes?"

That seemed like an odd division. "What are you getting at?"

"Maybe that's the killer's criteria. He's focusing on the quality-of-life issue. The terminal patients were facing a life of pain with death being the reward at the end of the road. The others, although not terminal, were just marking time until they died, because everyone regarded them as useless. They'd been abandoned by their families, or never had any. The quality of their lives wasn't very good, either."

The more she spoke, the more excited she became until the excitement all but radiated from her like beams of light. And that in turn, heaven help him, excited him as much as the theory she was advancing

"What if," she continued, her voice rising, "the killer isn't killing his victims out of some kind of sense of hatred but out of some kind of misguided sense of mercy?"

"Mercy?" he repeated. The moment he said it, more pieces fell into place. "You mean like an angel of mercy?" Cole asked incredulously. "Instead of an angel of death?"

"Why not? It wouldn't be the first time something like this happened—not at Patience Memorial," she was quick to clarify, "but it has happened before at other facilities. I remember reading something about that in the last six months, but I don't recall where. That guy managed to amass twenty-three dead people before anyone caught on." Her eyes met his. "And they only came up with that figure after they caught him in the act and wound up tracing his work history. He'd left a trail of dead people in his wake."

Cole nodded, thinking. She was onto something. "All right, why don't we see if any of the staff that's currently working in the Geriatrics Unit formerly worked at some other hospital or extended care facility where an unusual number of patients died." He knew he should be spreading his net wider, but for now, he was hoping that his grim reaper was operating on a small basis—and alone.

"How approachable is the head of Human Resources at your hospital?" Cole asked.

"Depends," she allowed, leaning a hip against his absent partner's desk. "You smile at her the way you just did at me and she'll be eating out of your hand," Nika promised. "I guarantee it."

"I was smiling at you?" he asked innocently.

"Yup."

Rising, Cole pulled her to him. "That's probably because I was thinking of the way we're going to spend the rest of the evening," he told her. "Especially the end of it."

She brushed her lips against his quickly. "Yes, me, too."

A tingle zigzagged through her. Judging by the look in his eyes, she wasn't experiencing that tingle alone.

It was hard to believe that this was the same no-nonsense detective who'd rescued her a little over two weeks ago.

What was even harder to imagine, Nika acknowledged sadly, was what life was going to be like without him in it.

Because she knew she'd be a fool to believe in happily-ever-after in this case. She knew, logically, that it wasn't going to happen. Cole Baker was a loner. He'd all but rented a billboard in Times Square telling her so.

So she didn't think beyond the parameters of the day and refused to allow her mind to wander toward tomorrow.

Chapter 13

Cole supposed that, in an odd way, he should be grateful that his crime scenes and the hospital where his grandmother was to have her biopsy had fortuitously turned out to be one and the same place.

Although dealing with his emotions, much less displaying them, had not been easy for him in almost two decades, he did want to be there for the woman. Or if not "there," meaning right outside the O.R., then at least somewhere within shouting distance so that he could be quickly located if need be. He knew that logically it didn't matter in the grand scheme of things, but it mattered to him. And, he knew, it mattered to his grandmother, even though she didn't come right out and say it.

They were shorthanded on the force and he already knew without asking that he couldn't get any time off. The detective who had been lent to Homicide from another department was now out with the flu, and his own partner hadn't fully recovered yet. Most likely because he'd refused to surrender to the inevitable in the first place. The man had hung on as long as he could before his weakened immune system had finally succumbed. The last time he'd seen his partner leaving the squad room, he'd looked like death warmed over.

Since he was spending so much time in the Geriatric Department, each day he came he had to be subjected to a quick once-over to make sure he wasn't displaying any symptoms of the flu.

The first time this happened Nika had explained to him that only people who'd already had the flu this year were allowed to be on the floor. It gave the patients on the geriatric floor one less thing to worry about.

He'd noted more than once she was very protective of these old people. The same could also be said of the rest of the staff. At one point or other he'd observed them all as they went about their duties.

So who the hell was doing away with the patients, and how was he or she doing it amid all these eyes that seemed to be trained on each patient?

How?

When?

Who?

The questions swam around in his head, all but haunting him. He had no answers.

He'd told his captain that he would be conducting interviews with each member of the staff who was currently on duty. This was intended not only to gather what could be important information but to trip up the killer somehow.

Those were his intentions, but once he arrived at the

hospital, Cole couldn't seem to focus on his job. This was the morning that G was having her biopsy. So he went to her room to be with her until it was time for her to be taken to the O.R.

As the minute hand raced behind the second hand, wantonly flinging away the minutes that remained before G's surgery, it became increasingly more difficult for him to concentrate.

"You coming down with something, Coleman?" Ericka finally asked, squinting at him through her state-of-the-art bifocals that she so dearly loved.

When he'd discovered how much she favored the glasses, he had secretly paid for the pair. They had set him back a bit, but it was worth it to see her pleasure. Her pride wouldn't have allowed him to pick up the tab. So he'd gone behind her back, paid for them and told the receptionist to tell his grandmother that Medicare had actually paid the bill in its entirety.

It was apparent that G had found the whole thing highly suspect, but she'd let it go. They didn't speak about it.

There were a lot of things that they didn't speak about, a lot that went unsaid between them. That didn't mean he didn't love her the way he'd vowed not to love anyone ever again. And, he was certain, G loved him, though she hardly ever used the L-word.

"Just working hard," Cole said, answering her question about his health.

He could tell she didn't believe him. "You don't have to hang around until they take me, you know," she told him. It wasn't the first time she'd said that this morning, though if it was because she was just repeating herself or because she didn't remember saying it, he didn't know.

He didn't want to think about that now, about the possibility of dementia stealing her from him. He didn't want to think about losing G on any level.

"Can't get rid of me that easily," he told her. Wandering over to the window, he pretended to look out. Rain slid down the pane. Weatherman hadn't mentioned rain for today. Being a weatherman had to be the cushiest job in the world, he mused.

"Tell me about it," Ericka snorted, doing her best to sound put-upon. "I saw you tiptoeing into my room last night, hovering over me. You thought I was asleep because it was so late, but I wasn't. Don't you have anything better to do with your time than to hover over me?"

Cole eyed her sharply, wondering if she was misremembering or just imagining things. Or if it was something else. "I came by last night with Dr. Pulaski," he reminded her. But that was early in the evening. "Is that what you're referring—"

"No." She cut him off. "This was later. The lights were dim in the hall, so it had to be after eleven," she remembered. "I didn't have my glasses on so I couldn't see what time it was, but it was definitely after you came by here with the baby doctor."

He stared at her for a moment, wondering if she was having one of her "hazy" moments, where information fled from her brain like floodwaters over the top of a reservoir.

"Dr. Pulaski works in geriatrics, not pediatrics," he corrected his grandmother.

"Not *baby* doctor," Ericka said, annoyed that he didn't understand. "*Baby* doctor." Then, because he still didn't look like he understood, Ericka went into detail. "She hardly looks old enough to have graduated high school, let alone medical school." And then Ericka shrugged petulantly. "'Course, at my age, everyone looks like a baby," she complained. "But you came back here without her and you hovered," she insisted. "You were trying to fool around with my IV, but then that nurse with the tight uniform came in." She laughed. "You dropped your hands to your sides like you used to do whenever I caught you getting into the cookie jar before dinner."

"Sure you weren't dreaming?" Cole asked. An eerie sensation shimmied up his spine.

Ericka drew herself up in bed, insulted. "I'm sure. Dreams don't smell," she added haughtily.

His eyes narrowed as he watched her. Understanding the woman was becoming more and more of a challenge. "Do you want to explain that one, G?"

His grandmother exhaled loudly, the way she always did when she was running out of patience.

"You had some god-awful aftershave on. It wasn't the kind that could make you gag half a room away, but up close and personal, well, that was a whole different story." Screwing up her face as if she was bracing for an ordeal, Ericka took in a deep breath, then nodded, her face relaxing. "Good, you threw the bottle away," she declared happily because there was no scent of any kind of cologne evident. "And if you didn't," she cautioned bluntly, "you should. Clean's the best kind of smell for a man."

"I'll try to remember that," he murmured, his mind racing, trying to integrate the information his grandmother had just given him.

It could all be nothing, and then again, with his grandmother winking in and out of her head on occasion, maybe she'd mistaken another man for him. A man who, from the sound of it, had been trying to do something with her IV line when someone else has come into the room, forcing him to stop whatever it was that he had been trying to do.

Something he wasn't supposed to do, because why else would he drop his hands to his sides?

"Ready?" Nika asked her patient cheerfully as she breezed into the room, dressed head to toe in blue scrubs. Glancing at Cole's expression caused the smile on her lips to freeze. "Is something wrong?" she asked him in as upbeat a voice as she could manage, for her patient's sake.

It was Ericka, not Cole, who answered her. "You mean other than the fact that I could die on the table? No," Ericka retorted. "Nothing's wrong."

Nika looked at the woman, giving her a kindly smile. "You're not going to die on the table, or anywhere else, Mrs. Baker."

Unconvinced—and desperately wanting to be— Ericka snorted. "You're going to make me all better, right?"

"Right," Nika assured her cheerfully. "I am. Along with Dr. Chase and eventually, Dr. Goodfellow. We're all going to work to make you good as new." Leaning over, she patted the woman's hand. "Maybe even better than new."

Ericka's sharp blue eyes regarded her for a long moment. And then she declared, "Whatever you're smoking or drinking, I want them to use it for my anesthesia."

The woman was something else, all right. Nika exchanged glances with Cole before she told her patient, "I doubt very much if they're going to put orange juice into your veins, Mrs. Baker, because that's what I'm drinking. And I don't smoke." She heard the rest of the support team entering behind her. "Okay, time for your magic carpet ride to begin." She stepped back as the orderly and nurse approached the hospital bed. "Gerald and Jenna are going to take you down to the O.R.," she told the woman.

Ericka grabbed her wrist. A flicker of fear flashed in her eyes. "I thought you were coming with me."

Nika gave Ericka's hand a squeeze, gently separating the woman's fingers from her wrist.

"I'll be there," Nika promised. "They're going to prep you first."

Ericka looked at the orderly, who responded with an encouraging smile. Ericka didn't smile back. "As long as he doesn't get fresh."

"I'll be the one getting you ready, Mrs. Baker," Jenna spoke up as she positioned herself at the foot of the hospital bed. One hand on the footboard, ready to guide it out, she nodded at the orderly. The burly man kicked away the brakes on all four wheels and began to push. The bed glided out of the room and into the hallway.

"What's wrong?" Nika asked Cole the moment everyone had left the room.

He wasn't aware that his expression had given anything away. "Maybe nothing."

Was that a faint hint of aftershave he'd just smelled? Or was that a woman's cologne? He was letting his imagination run away with him—not a normal occurrence. Cole struggled to rein it in.

He hadn't said "nothing," he'd said "maybe nothing." Nika wanted to hear what the "maybe" was all about. "But...?" she pressed.

For a moment Cole thought of keeping this to himself, then decided that maybe he could use her input. "G thinks I was in her room last night."

Was that all? Had he forgotten? "You were. We both were, remember?"

He shook his head. "No, she means afterwards. She claims she woke up to find me hovering over her, fiddling around with her IV."

Nika knew that wasn't possible. He'd spent the night with her. Concerned, Nika tried to think how they could find out if the woman had dreamed the whole thing, or if there'd actually been someone in her room. Someone who at least vaguely resembled Cole.

"Did you check the surveillance tapes from the hall for last night?"

"No, but I intend to as soon as possible." Cole schooled himself not to make too much of it, just in case. "She might just be imagining it. Her mind does wander off at times," he said. Using the euphemism "wander" was his way of dealing with the possibility of Alzheimer's.

One possible crisis at a time.

"She also said she thought it was me," he reminded Nika. "And we both know that I wasn't anywhere near her late last night." He watched her pointedly, replaying some of the moments they'd shared in his head. "I was with you."

"Very much so," Nika agreed, smiling broadly at him. Their lovemaking just seemed to get better and better, even though at the outset, she couldn't see how that was possible. She reined in her thoughts and focused on his grandmother. "Seems like too much of a coincidence to think she just dreamed the whole thing."

"There's something else," he said. "G told me she smelled my cologne and that it was too strong. I don't wear cologne. The logical conclusion would be that she dreamed this."

Nika reconsidered his theory. "It's a possibility," she allowed. "Dreams do come in all sorts of sizes and shapes. I've had some incredibly vivid dreams." The most recent one had been about him, but she wasn't ready to admit that to him yet. "I can't see why smells and even taste can't be part of that vivid experience." She needed to start scrubbing in, but she hated the idea of leaving him alone to wait for his grandmother's surgery to be over. "Are you going to hang around while she's in the O.R.?" she asked, then subtly tried to get him to go back to work. In the long run, that would be better for him than just waiting here. "When she comes out, your grandmother won't be conscious. She won't know if you're not here."

"No, she won't," he agreed. "But I will."

Nika walked out of the room, making her way to the elevator. He fell into step beside her. "Tell you what— I'll text you the second she's out of surgery."

They turned a corner. He allowed himself a small smile. "Trying to get rid of me?"

Her mission was loftier than that. "Trying to get you to relax and breathe regularly. Really, you don't need to hang around here." Reaching the elevator, she pressed the down button, then turned to face him. "Keeping busy is the best way to make time pass," she said. "Go, be super-detective. Find out who's behind all this," she requested earnestly. "Please. Before we lose someone else."

In the face of everything, it was not an unreasonable request. And Veronika was right, he thought. He was better off keeping busy.

The elevator arrived. The car was empty as she stepped into it. He suddenly remembered what he wanted to tell her. "Oh, don't text me," he told her, stopping the doors with his hand before they closed and the elevator whisked her away. The doors instantly sprang back.

This time Nika placed her hand in the way as she looked at him, curious. "You don't want to know?"

Cole shook his head. "It's not that. Call me instead."

He didn't elaborate. He didn't have to. Nika put two and two together and grinned. The man had made no secret of his dislike of all things technological. "You don't have to know how to send a text in order to be able to read one."

Cole had never liked owning up to any shortcomings and, in this day and age, not being able to communicate on all levels was considered a basic shortcoming. But if he didn't say something, he had a feeling that Nika would go on and on about it.

"I don't know how to access a text message."

She opened her mouth both to instruct him and to laugh at the look on Cole's face. But then she decided to do neither. This wasn't the time to tease him. So instead, she merely nodded.

"Then I'll call you with any news," she promised. She took away her hand from the spasmodically shrugging elevator doors. The doors dived toward each other. "Now go, make the world safe," she ordered a second before the doors finally shut.

She was only half teasing.

The mass in Ericka Baker's breast turned out to be deeper than the MRI had led them to believe. Consequently, the procedure lasted longer than had initially been estimated. And rather than just performing a needle biopsy, Dr. Chase opted then and there to remove the entire mass. A small section of the tissue was immediately sent off to the pathology lab.

Nika mentally crossed her fingers and offered up a quick, silent prayer that the results would be benign. She'd grown to like the feisty little octogenarian a great deal since she'd first met Ericka Baker.

When the procedure was over, Nika had walked beside the gurney, accompanying the unconscious woman to the Recovery Room. She checked Ericka's vital signs even before the on-duty nurse arrived to take them. Anxious to set his mind at ease as much as possible, Nika wanted to be able to give Cole all the information she could. So far, it was all good.

She fervently hoped it would remain that way.

Leaving her patient with the recovery room nurse, who, not counting Mrs. Baker, had six other patients to watch over in the small, antiseptic and darkened room, Nika stepped out into the hall.

She blinked a couple of times to get her eyes accustomed to the brighter lighting. Once the halos receded from around certain fixtures, Nika went in search of a landline. Her cell phone was still in her locker where she'd left after changing into her blue O.R. scrubs.

She found one next to the ladies' room opposite Outpatient Admitting.

She didn't bother to change now beyond removing her mask and surgical cap, which somehow *always* felt too small every time she put it on—Alyx claimed it was because she had such an incredibly big head. Nika dialed Cole's cell number.

It took her two tries to get through. The first time his cell phone aborted midway, losing the signal. But her second attempt reached him. She listened to the phone ring and began counting in her head.

Cole's crisp baritone rang in her ear as he answered his phone on the third ring. "Baker."

She wondered if her stomach would ever stop tightening at the sound of his voice. "Cole, it's Nika—"

She could almost feel him gripping the phone tightly as he asked her in a stony voice, obviously braced for the worst, "How is she?"

Nika talked quickly, not wanting to prolong his anxiety one second longer than she had to. "Your grandmother came through the procedure with flying colors."

It was only then that he let out the breath he'd been holding for the last hour and ten minutes.

"Why did it take so long?" he asked.

He'd been acutely aware of the time and that Nika hadn't gotten in contact with him as she'd promised. Aware as well that the surgery had gone over the time parameters she'd given him.

She gave him the whole story, hoping it would make him feel more comfortable about the operation. "The doctor decided to take out the whole mass instead of just aspirating it. A section of it was sent to the pathology lab for a workup." Nika anticipated his next question. "We should know one way or another in about forty-eight hours, if not sooner." She heard Cole sigh and she could just guess what was going on in his head. In his place, she'd feel the same way. "I know, I know, more waiting, but just think of it as no news being good news."

He made a dismissive noise. "Sorry, I never went to the Pollyanna School of Optimism. No news is almost always bad news waiting to happen."

How could he stand to live that way, she wondered. It was so bleak.

"Cole, your grandmother is going to be all right. You have to believe that. For her sake if not for your own," she emphasized. She took the silence on the other end of the line to be skepticism and continued. "She's a sharp little old lady. If you're standing there, looking at her as if you've already paid for the funeral casket and the service, I guarantee she'll pick up on it. Cole, she needs all the positive energy she can get. She needs you to be positive for her. Positive that she's going to be all right."

There was more silence on the other end, and for a second she thought that he'd either lost the signal again or he'd hung up on her.

"Cole?"

When he spoke, his tone was only a shade less serious than it had been a moment ago. "So now you're a motivational speaker, too?"

Nika couldn't tell if he was being sarcastic, or this was his poor attempt at humor. In either case, her answer was the same. "I'm whatever I have to be in order to help my patients."

"Yeah, I know," he conceded. "So when can I see my grandmother?"

"I just brought her into the Recovery Room. She's going to be there for another hour and then, if everything's okay—and it has been up to this point," she added in case he was already assuming that it wasn't, "they'll take her back up to her room. So, to answer your question, if you can get back to the hospital, you can see her in about an hour."

"I don't have to 'get back,'" he told her. "I never left the Geriatrics Unit."

Chapter 14

Nika shifted the phone to her other ear and turned away from the general flow of foot traffic in order to focus better on the sound of his voice. If he was on the premises, but not down here, there was only one reason for that.

"I take it you're talking to the staff up there."

Because he was so straightforward, Nika didn't know if his talking to the staff without her present was such a good thing. She at least could smooth the feathers that Cole might inadvertently be ruffling with his no-nonsense approach to questioning. Right now, they needed all the cooperation from the people in the unit they could get. She didn't want him alienating anyone. Geriatrics couldn't afford to lose anyone, and this included the nurses and the orderlies.

"Seems like the logical thing to do," Cole told her. There was no emotion in his voice.

"I know, but I really can't picture any of them doing away with our patients for *any* reason," Nika emphasized.

"You know them that well?" he questioned.

She could hear the skepticism in his voice and knew without asking what he was thinking: How well did anyone ever know anyone else? While he might have a point, she liked to believe that she was a fairly decent judge of character.

"Actually, in terms of longevity, I'm practically the last one hired on the floor." She wanted to discuss this further with him and she didn't want to do it over the phone. "Look, stay where you are, I'm coming up."

"Aren't you needed in the Recovery Room?" he asked.

It wasn't the Recovery Room he was thinking about, Nika thought. It was his grandmother. Not that she could fault him. When her mother went in for gall bladder surgery two years ago, she'd been the same way. Worried, concerned, keeping vigil at the woman's bedside even though her mother was asleep for most of the twenty-four hours that followed the surgery. Even so, rather than leave, she remained. It made her feel better just watching her mother breathe. Besides, her sisters were depending on her to give them periodic updates since all three of them were unable to get to the hospital until the next day.

Rather than tiptoeing around his concern and allowing him to keep his stoic facade, Nika told him, "Your grandmother's resting comfortably and there's really nothing for me to do except take her vitals every fifteen minutes. The on-duty nurse is going to think I'm after her job if I do it again. Stay put," she instructed a second time. "I'll be right there." With that, she ended the call.

The bank of elevators was less than ten feet away, but filled with nervous energy that she couldn't quite shake and her recent period of captivity in the elevator car still very fresh in her mind, Nika opted to take the stairs.

She all but ran up the three flights of metal stairs, the heels of her shoes beating a rhythmic sound as she hurried to the fourth floor.

She was a little breathless and her cheeks were flushed as she pushed opened the stairwell door. She'd emerged on the far end of the floor where some of the supplies were kept. There was no one around. Nika assumed that Cole was at the nurses' station, which served as an oasis for charts, computers and the all-important coffeemaker that kept them all fully functional. The nurses' station was located in the center of each floor.

But Cole wasn't at the nurses' station.

Still unaccountably antsy, Nika began a cursory search for the detective, making her way to the opposite end of the floor. She glanced into every room she passed. More than half were occupied, but Cole wasn't in any of them.

She finally found him standing before the bank of regular elevators. She should have realized he'd be here, she silently upbraided herself.

Coming up behind Cole, she told him, "I took the stairs."

Cole instantly swung around. There was a tension in his face she'd never seen before. Was he that worried about his grandmother, or was something else going on?

"Never sneak up on a cop with a gun," Cole warned her.

"I wasn't sneaking," Nika protested. *Was* there something wrong? "Next time, I'll remember to bring some pots and pans with me and drop them before I say anything."

"Sarcasm," he pronounced, his eyes flat, unfathomable as they delved into her. And then he nodded. "I like it."

Nika shook her head, the corners of her mouth curving softly. "You are a strange, strange man, Detective Cole Baker."

"Nice of you to notice," he quipped.

There was even a hint of a smile on his lips. Maybe she'd been mistaken about the tension, she thought. Being intimate with him didn't automatically mean that she was privy to his thoughts or to his soul. She could only wish that she was.

"So how many of the staff did you get to talk to?" she asked casually. On the plus side, she hadn't seen a mass exodus underway. Maybe he'd learned tact in the last two weeks.

"All of them."

She hadn't been gone that long. He must have been into speed interviews. But then, if everyone was innocent, it would stand to reason that the interviews would be over quickly, she judged.

"Impressive. I underestimated your zeal. Did you find out anything?" she asked, trying to sound as casual as she could, considering that she had a vested interest in finding this maniac.

"No." And it didn't take a psychiatrist to see that the lack of results really got under his skin. "They all seem upset at the thought that it might be one of their own doing the killing, but at the same time, they're eager to help bring an end to this."

Amen to that, she thought. "I told you. They're good people."

He nodded dismissively. "On the surface."

She could have expected nothing different from him. "And you're digging, right?"

"As fast as I can," he answered. Even though it wasn't fast enough to suit him, he added silently. "I'm having Calvin run all their social security numbers through every databank we have access to. Something's got to come up." He seemed to have no doubts about that.

Logic dictated that he was right. But she didn't deal in logic alone.

"Calvin?" she asked. She would have remembered if he'd mentioned that name before. It sounded like something from the last century.

"The precinct's resident computer whiz kid. Turns out he's the captain's nephew." He'd stumbled across that little piece of information by accident. It wasn't something that either Calvin or his uncle advertised. "For once, nepotism is actually working out. Cal can practically make a computer dance on its hind legs."

"A computer doesn't have hind legs," she pointed out tactfully.

"That's why the trick is so impressive," he deadpanned.

The man had a sense of humor. There was hope for the universe yet. Whether that meant hope for them or not was another story, one she didn't have time to explore right now, Nika told herself. Right now, she was a doctor. Later she'd be the woman whose kneecaps melted every time Cole Baker came within breathing distance.

"Has this Calvin person found anything of interest?" she asked.

That was where his testy mood was coming from. "Other than one of the nurses' arrest for shoplifting years ago, nothing so far."

"Shoplifting?" Nika echoed, stunned. She couldn't envision any of the nurses she'd been working with taking anything that didn't belong to them beyond perhaps a Post-it note. "Who?"

But Cole shook his head. "Sorry, those records are sealed."

The hell they were. "But this Calvin obviously hacked into them and he told you."

"He did," Cole agreed. "But this is on a need-to-know basis."

"And I need to know," she shot back. She needed to know about the people she worked next to. Needed to know their weaknesses and their strengths—and whether or not they had ever run afoul of authority.

Cole saw no reason for her to have the information. "The woman shoplifted some makeup from a department store counter, she didn't electrocute the undercover floor walker. And it was years ago, when she was a kid."

"You're not going to tell me." It wasn't a question on her part, it was an annoyed conclusion. And, as it turned out, the right one.

"Nope."

And he wouldn't, no matter how hard she tried to get it out of him. She knew that without being told. He was protecting the rights of a tarnished soul. Noble.

Who would have thought?

Nika sighed. "You are one hard man to figure out." She laughed shortly. "Of course, they say that once the mystery's gone, the relationship is doomed." He looked at her sharply the moment she uttered the word "relationship." "Not that we have one," she quickly added. She didn't want him to feel as if she was hemming him in or even attempting to label what was happening between them.

"We don't."

It was actually a question, but at the last minute, he stopped himself from using an inflection in his tone that would turn it into one. It was obvious by her denial that she didn't want a relationship, he thought. He didn't need to be hit over the head to realize that.

He knew he should be happy. Or, at the very least, since "happy" was a stretch for him, he should feel relieved. She wasn't asking for anything, certainly not a commitment. Most women after they'd slept with someone more than twice wanted the future spelled out, clarified and plotted out to infinity.

Yet she didn't.

Why?

Didn't what they had going on between them matter to her?

That had to be it. Again, he waited for the relief to come. It didn't.

Nika pressed her lips together. She couldn't figure out if he'd just asked her a question, or made a statement that was ultimately agreeing with what she'd arbitrarily thrown out into the conversation, mainly to see his reaction.

It's the latter, you idiot.

She'd known from the beginning that Cole didn't

want to have a lasting relationship. That whatever was going on between them was going to defy labels and remain in the realm of the unknown, to be taken one moment at a time and nothing more. It had no past and no future. It just was. Until the day came that it wasn't.

It was as simple and as complex as that.

At a loss as to how to respond to this awkward estrangement that had come in from nowhere and instantly taken hold, Nika was rescued by Sally, one of the day-shift nurses.

Tall, willowy and blond, Sally Nelson cheerfully thrust a coffee container covered in light blue contact paper between them. The container was filled with dollar bills and change. She shook it slightly for emphasis.

"I'm taking up a collection," she needlessly announced.

"For?" Nika asked when nothing more enlightening followed the declaration.

"It's for a going-away gift for Gerald—the orderly," Sally added as if to distinguish him from all the other Geralds, except that there weren't any.

The announcement had immediately snagged Cole's attention. "He's leaving?"

The nurse bobbed her head up and down. "He has to," Sally answered, her sunny expression giving way to one that was borderline serious. "His mother's not doing well and he told us that he's going to have to go on an indefinite leave of absence because he wants to take care of her full-time."

"What does he plan to do for money?" Cole asked. Taking care of an infirm senior citizen required a great deal of capital.

Sally laughed and waved her hand at the question,

dismissing it. "Oh, Gerald doesn't need to worry about that. He says his father left his mother really well-off. The old man had this huge insurance policy when he died. His mother was going to use the money to move into one of those assisted living homes, but Gerald told her he wouldn't hear of it. What kind of a son would he be, he said, letting strangers take care of her when he was actually trained to do that kind of thing himself?"

"Very noble of him," Cole commented in a flat voice.

Nika took out her wallet and tossed in a ten, which brought Sally's smile back, increasing its wattage by a third. Turning away from the nurse, Nika lowered her voice and said to Cole, "You're being sarcastic."

"Was I?" he asked. "I thought that was my regular speaking voice."

"It was," she acknowledged, the corners of her mouth curving, "but it was still sarcastic. You think Gerald's volunteering to take care of his mother to keep her from spending the proceeds from the life insurance policy, don't you?"

"Greed does make the world go around," he told her simply, then added, "But I don't believe anything until I check it out." Even as he said it, he was taking out his cell phone.

The way Cole said the last part made her feel uneasy. Suspicious. She put her hand on his wrist to keep him from making the call he was obviously anxious to place.

"Does that apply to everyone?" she asked. "Do you always check everything and everyone out?" Before he could answer, she demanded, "Did you check me out?"

She had no idea why that upset her as much as it did, but it did. She supposed that it made her feel as if he regarded her the same way he regarded everyone else.

While she subconsciously knew that it was probably true, that she was no different from anyone else to him, she didn't want to be forced to face the evidence, at least, not yet. Not until she'd psyched herself up a little more.

"Yes, I did," he told her after a beat. He didn't see why this would upset her, especially considering his timing. "That was when your hospital administrator was ready to lay you on the sacrificial altar as the prime suspect in these less-than-natural deaths that keep occurring in your unit. I'm the one who cleared you, remember? That required checking you out. I couldn't just look into your eyes and pronounce you innocent."

Although, he had to admit, albeit only to himself, something in her eyes had made him believe in her innocence to begin with. Knowing that he'd find proof to substantiate it just helped.

"I know," she said, but he picked up on the fact that she seemed far from pleased about his honesty.

Damn, but women were just too complicated a species to get caught up with, Cole thought. Served him right for letting his guard down and allowing himself to stumble away from his very well-defined path. He was a loner and loners didn't get caught up in eyes the color of the sky, or lips that tasted of vanilla or killer legs that went on forever. Loners remained alone. It was a self-explanatory definition.

Nika drew her shoulders back, a soldier braced to do her duty.

"I'd better go back downstairs and see if your grandmother's ready to be moved back up to her room," she told him.

What she didn't add was that she wanted to put a little distance between them until she could come to grips with this glaring reminder she'd just been given. A reminder that whatever she was secretly hoping they had going on between them, while not dead on arrival, was certainly not expected to have any kind of healthy, lengthy lifespan.

Cole nodded in response. Wanting to go downstairs with Nika to see his grandmother, he knew he needed to follow up on this new piece of information. When he'd initially interviewed the friendly orderly, the man had made no mention that he was thinking of leaving the hospital any time in the near future.

He supposed that Gerald might not have thought it was relevant, but in his experience, it was always the seemingly irrelevant pieces of information that usually broke a case.

Cole hoped like hell that lightning would strike again.

Going to his grandmother's room, he crossed to the window—the area he'd accidentally discovered had the best reception for his cell phone—and made his call.

Dialing the number to the precinct, he didn't bother listening to the recorded voice that was prompting him to pay attention to the menu "as it has changed." Instead, he tapped out the extension he needed.

The phone on the other end rang three times before the receiver was picked up. Cole didn't wait for the computer tech to announce himself. Instead, he dived right into the call.

"Cal, Baker," he made the introduction quickly. "Did you have a chance to look into more of Gerald Mayfield's background yet?" Taking a worn notepad out of his back pocket, he flipped it open, then found what he was looking for. For good measure, Cole rattled off the social security number he'd jotted down next to the orderly's name. "You did?" Cole warned himself not to expect too much. He was probably just on a wild-goose chase. More than likely, the orderly was clean. "Okay, what did you find out?"

The rather high voice on the other end began to review his recent findings. "Mayfield's worked for several nursing homes since he graduated from a two-year college fifteen years ago. They all raved about how good he was with patients. There's a bunch of glowing references in his HR file."

Damn. But then, Cole reminded himself, references could be forged. "Check those out for me, see if they're legitimate. And what about the stats at these places? Did any of these nursing homes experience a higher than usual mortality rate when compared to other, similar facilities?"

"Nothing that stands out at first glance," Calvin told him. "But I could dig a little deeper if you want."

"I want," Cole told him firmly. "And while you're at it, see if you can find out how big his father's insurance policy was."

There was a momentary pause on the other end. "What insurance policy?"

At this point, Cole had no idea what insurance company had issued the policy. "The one he had in force when he died. I'm assuming that wasn't all that long ago."

"There wasn't any," Cal assured him. "And I don't know what you mean by 'all that long ago,' but the old man's ticker gave out ten years ago. According to what the doctor wrote in his chart, Gerald Mayfield's father died of a broken heart because he couldn't live without his wife."

Cole's head snapped up. "Mayfield's mother is dead?"

"Yup. Has been for ten years. Died less than six months before her husband. Why?"

"Because Mayfield said he was leaving the hospital to devote himself to taking care of his mother." *Bingo!* "I think we just found our guy." He cautioned himself not to get overconfident just yet. There could still be some sort of an explanation, although he didn't see how. "Get back to me with that information," he instructed. With that, he terminated his call.

Hurrying back to the nurses' station, he saw that Sally, the nurse with the paper-wrapped tin can, was the only one there. Cole pressed his card into her hand. "Call me the second Gerald Mayfield turns up. And don't let him go into a patient's room unsupervised."

Sally rose in her chair, confused. "Why?"

He didn't have time to explain. "Just do it," he told her, running toward the stairwell.

Before entering, he called Nika on her cell. He wanted to warn her to stay clear of the orderly.

Nika wasn't picking up.

Chapter 15

When Nika didn't pick up the third time he tried calling her, Cole told himself that there was no reason to let his imagination get the better of him. Her cell phone was probably still in her locker, where she'd put it when she'd changed into scrubs for his grandmother's surgery.

That was what he told himself, but that wasn't what he actually believed.

His mind told him one thing, casting its vote on the side of logic. His gut went a whole different route. It told him she was in trouble.

There was no doubt that what he'd just discovered about the departing orderly colored his judgment, but Cole definitely had a bad feeling about this. A bad feeling that had him heading for the stairwell and the Recovery Room on the first floor.

Nika stared at the Recovery Room nurse, stunned. A very uneasy feeling was spreading out all through her. "What do you mean Gerald came and got Mrs. Baker?"

"He came and got her," the woman repeated. It was clear that she didn't see what the problem was.

Granted, this wasn't the ideal time to carry on a conversation, at least as far as the nurse was probably concerned. At the moment, Judy pretty much had her hands full, so to speak. One of the post-op patients had suddenly woken up ahead of schedule, obviously urged on by the churning sensation in her stomach.

At present, the groggy, moaning woman was throwing up into the pink plastic container that Judy was holding up to her mouth. The intense, nauseating smell that emerged was enough to drive anyone from the room. But Cole's grandmother was missing and Nika needed this cleared up—as in fifteen minutes ago.

"By whose authority?" she demanded. Orderlies didn't just come waltzing into the Recovery Room and whisk post-op patients away at whim.

The beleaguered nurse looked at Nika as if she'd suddenly raffled away her mind. "Yours," she answered tersely.

Nika blinked. That wasn't possible. She hadn't authorized anything. "Excuse me?"

"Gerald said that you'd told him to bring Mrs. Baker back to her room, and that you would watch her for a while as a favor to that detective. She's his grandmother, right?"

"Right." Frustrated, she wasn't even sure where to begin. "But I didn't—" Nika regrouped and tried again. "Didn't you think that was a little odd, his coming here and just commandeering the woman on my supposed say-so?"

Judy appeared torn between the question and holding her patient's head. "It's not my place to think anything's odd. I just go by the rules unless I'm told otherwise. Keep a low profile, keep your job," Judy recited in a singsong voice.

Considering the state of the economy of late, Nika could understand where the nurse was coming from. But even so, there was such a thing as making sure all actions were on the level. Why hadn't she just stopped to check by placing a call to the Geriatrics Unit?

With a sigh, Nika focused on her next move, finding Gerald before, God forbid, the orderly did something that couldn't be undone.

"How long ago was he here?" It couldn't have been *that* long ago, she reasoned, because she'd been down here less than half an hour ago.

Judy set down the plastic tub and shrugged. "Five, ten minutes, something like that." She barely disguised her annoyance. "I wasn't timing it."

Nika was having trouble hanging on to her temper. "Which way did he go?"

"Through the doors," the nurse retorted, then added impatiently, "and into the elevator, I guess." The patient began making gagging noises again. Judy grabbed the container and held it up for the woman. When she spoke, the nurse hardly sounded like herself. She was trying to talk without inhaling. "What's the big deal?" she asked.

The answer would have to wait. Nika was already hurrying out of the dim room, pushing open the doors with both hands. She made a beeline for the first phone she saw. It was on the corner of the hospitality receptionist's desk.

Dispensing with formalities, Nika snatched up the

receiver and started dialing. "I need to make a call to the Geriatrics Unit," Nika said when the woman looked at her in surprise. "It's urgent."

She shifted her weight from foot to foot, impatiently waiting for the on-duty nurse to pick up. It felt like two eternities had gone by before she heard a female voice on the line. "Geriatrics, this is Sally."

"Sally, this is Dr. Pulaski. Did Gerald come up with Mrs. Baker yet?" She crossed her fingers, hoping for a positive answer. Hoping that she was just overreacting and that the orderly was just trying to be helpful. He always had been before.

"No," the nurse answered, turning the single syllable word into one that had several syllables at its disposal.

"Are you sure?" Nika stressed.

"Of course I'm sure. I've got an unobstructed view of Mrs. Baker's room from here. Gerald didn't come back with her. She's not in her bed." And then she made a funny little noise as she remembered something. "Oh, that cute detective wanted me to tell you—"

But Nika had already hung up.

Where could the orderly have gone with Mrs. Baker, and why? At this point, the "why" seemed rather obvious, but she didn't want to believe it. Gerald Mayfield was one of the most cheerful, most dedicated people she'd ever met. Try as she might to recall otherwise, she'd never seen the man without a smile on his face. Moreover, he was always looking to do more, to go not just the extra mile, but the entire distance if need be.

Could someone like that really be responsible for the recent rash of deaths?

She couldn't get herself to believe it—and yet, what else could she think? There was no reason for him to take it upon himself to remove a patient from the recovery area on his own—or to lie about it.

Right now she didn't need to think, Nika told herself. She needed to track the orderly down. He shouldn't be that difficult to find. It wasn't as if he could just disappear with Cole's grandmother. The man was pushing a gurney, for God sakes. How much more conspicuous could he be?

The line, "Hide in plain sight," flashed through her head. Seeing an orderly pushing a gurney with or without a patient in it was a common sight. No one would even notice.

Nika felt her heart inch its way up her throat. It wasn't the kind of lump that came about when someone was being sentimental. It was the kind that fairly screamed of fear.

Where had the orderly taken Cole's grandmother?

She tried to think like her quarry. If his intent was to eliminate the woman, his best bet was to do it in an unoccupied room. There simply weren't any on the first floor. All the O.R. suites were booked. That meant that Gerald had to have gone up to one of the other floors.

But which one?

For a split second, Nika thought of getting on the loudspeaker and paging him, but that would only alert him. Or maybe, please God, it would make him stop long enough for her to be able to catch up to him.

Still, she couldn't take that chance.

Going with her previous hunch, Nika began the search by dashing up the stairs to the second floor. Once there, she ran to the nurses' station.

"Did you see an orderly pushing a gurney with an unconscious old woman on it?" she asked eagerly.

God, did that ever sound melodramatic, she thought. Especially since she was breathing rather hard as she asked the question.

The nurse told her that she hadn't seen anyone pushing a gurney onto the floor. Gerald hadn't gotten off on the second floor.

She was about to run up to the next floor to ask the nurse there if she'd seen Gerald when it suddenly occurred to her where Gerald would have gone. It was the perfect place. The eighth floor could be counted on to have empty rooms. The floor was reserved for the wealthy and for visiting dignitaries who thought nothing of paying for the privilege of having a hospital room that could pass as one of the higher-end hotel suites.

Turning back to the nurse, she said, "Listen to me. I need you to call Detective Baker and tell him to meet me on the eighth floor." She rattled off Cole's cell number from memory quickly.

Confused, the nurse stared at her. "Who *are* you?"

"Dr. Pulaski. *Nika* Pulaski," she emphasized, since there were so many doctors in the hospital by that last name already. At last count, besides her, there were six. "Please tell him it's urgent."

The nurse obviously had her own interpretation of what she meant by the word "urgent." "If they catch you up there fooling around in one of the empty rooms, it's grounds for dismissal," the nurse warned her.

"How about if they catch me preventing a murder?" Nika countered.

The nurse's jaw dropped open and she immediately began dialing the number she'd been given.

Though she really didn't want to, Nika was forced to take the elevator. Eight floors were a bit too many to run up and still be of any kind of use once she reached the suites. She was tense the entire ride up.

She deliberately took the freight elevator, thinking that Gerald would want to avoid detection as much as he could. Getting off the elevator car, she braced herself and immediately began looking for the orderly and Cole's grandmother. There were twelve spacious suites on a floor that could have accommodated thirty single care units. Each suite had its door closed. Taking a deep breath, Nika started opening them, peering into each suite without first knocking or announcing herself. She didn't want Gerald forewarned.

She went through the first six in short order, finding two of the rooms occupied by patients who were less than pleased to be paying exorbitant fees just to have their privacy invaded. Nika left hasty apologies in her wake as she hurried to the next suite.

Disheartened, not to mention exceedingly worried, she started on the second six.

She found Gerald and Cole's grandmother in the next to the last suite on the floor.

Her heart hammering, she entered the room quietly. Even so, the orderly sensed her presence. She saw his shoulders instantly tensing the moment she eased the door open.

Her first thought was to keep him calm—and to buy time until Cole showed up.

In a gentle, soft voice, she asked, "What are you doing, Gerald? You got off on the wrong floor."

From what she could see, he was fussing with the IV drip, but it didn't appear that he'd taken it off the rack yet. "I'm taking care of Mrs. Baker. Making her comfortable."

"I'm her doctor, Gerald. I didn't leave any instructions for you to follow."

"Not your instructions I'm following," he told her, his tone mild. Distant.

"Then whose are they?" she asked, inching her way toward the orderly. At this proximity, she could see that he had a syringe in his hand.

Her heart began hammering harder. She was right. Gerald *was* the one killing the patients. But why?

She needed to distract him, to keep him from using that syringe.

"God's," he answered simply.

"God told you to kill those people?" Nikka kept her tone even, as if she was just trying to understand what he was telling her. She knew she needed to keep his confidence, to make him feel as if he could trust her.

The orderly nodded. It was clear by his manner that he felt he was doing something noble. Something sanctified.

"God doesn't like people to suffer." He was smiling as he looked down at the sleeping face of the woman he was determined to help find peace. "I'm separating them from their suffering."

Nikka took another small step forward. The orderly was taller and heavier than she was, but she was hoping that if she had to, she could literally throw him off balance. She'd have the element of surprise in her favor.

"Mrs. Baker isn't suffering," she pointed out softly.

"Oh, but she will be," he told her, his voice sorrowful, as if he could already feel the old woman's pain. "She'll suffer horribly. Once the cancer advances."

"We don't know that she does have cancer," Nika gently reminded him. "That's why the tissue sample was sent to the lab. So they could analyze it."

But Gerald shook his head. "It's cancer. I know it's cancer," he insisted. "I can tell."

She pretended to be impressed. "How can you tell, Gerald?"

His voice grew raspy as he recalled. "She looks just like my mother did when she came down with pancreatic cancer." There were tears in his eyes as he looked at Nika. "At the end, she begged me to kill her. I don't want Mrs. Baker to suffer like that." He brushed his hand along the woman's silver-gray hair. "I want her to go peacefully. She deserves that."

"What about Mr. Peters? He didn't have cancer. He wasn't dying of anything. Why did you pick him?" Nika tactfully used the word "pick" rather than "kill" because it was far less confrontational that way. She didn't want Gerald to become angry or defensive. She wanted him to think she was his friend.

The answer was the same. "To keep him from suffering," Gerald said.

Nika looked at him. It wasn't much of a stretch for her to pretend to be confused. "I don't understand."

Gerald sighed, as if he couldn't fathom why she didn't see what was so clear to him.

"Mr. Peters was being sent back to the nursing home. Do you know what those places are?" he demanded, a flash of anger in his eyes. "They're holding zones for people just waiting to die. He was a hero, a policeman who saved lives. He didn't deserve to be thrown aside like that. Like some rotten leftovers," he concluded bitterly. And then, just as suddenly as he'd scowled, Gerald was smiling again. "Now he's better off."

Somehow, she needed to get through to him. To make Gerald stop before he killed Cole's grandmother.

"You can't make those decisions for people, Gerald. I was going to help Mr. Peters find a roommate so he could share the expense of having his own place again."

"No, you weren't," the orderly accused petulantly. "You're just saying that to make me feel guilty. Well, it won't work! I saved Mr. Peters from suffering!" he insisted angrily.

Ignoring her now, Gerald began to uncouple the IV so that he could insert the syringe into it. The moment he took down the IV, Nika went to grab his wrist. Just then, she heard a noise behind her.

It all happened so fast that it was almost a blur. One moment, she was reaching for the orderly's wrist, the next, he'd yanked her off balance, and had a choke hold on her. With his arm around her throat, Nika felt as if the orderly was crushing her larynx as he dragged her to him, his eyes riveted to Cole.

She felt the sharp tip of the syringe against her neck. Nika had no doubt that he would use it. And if he did, she estimated that she was less than a handful of heartbeats away from death.

Cole had his weapon out, holding it with both his hands to keep it steady. The muzzle was aimed directly at the orderly's head.

"Let her go, Mayfield," he ordered.

"And have you kill me? Sorry, not really one of the better offers I've gotten. What I'm doing is right," he insisted, his voice sounding as if it was about to crack. "They don't suffer. They die with dignity, not rot away, piece by piece. Can't you understand that?" Gerald demanded angrily, then his eyes widened with determination, the hand with the syringe rising just a little, as if he was about to strike. "Come one step closer and I'll kill her."

It turned out to be the last thing he said.

Gerald died with a look of shock on his face, a single bullet hole right between his eyes.

"Don't move another step closer," Cole said at the same moment that he fired his gun. While he was in college, he'd never missed a Saturday at the firing range. Being a dead shot had been important to him. Now he realized why. It was as if fate had been preparing him for this one moment.

To save the woman who had, without his permission and almost without his knowledge, become so important to him.

Nika thought her legs had turned to liquid—until she used them to run from the crumpling body. Mercifully, they still worked.

"You got my message," she cried, relieved.

Rather than say something to confirm that, or to give voice to the fact that, quite possibly for the rest of his life, he would be grateful beyond words that he'd managed to save her in time, Cole vented the incredible swirling turmoil within him.

He exploded at her.

"Who the hell do you think you are, some kind of superhero? You can't just go running off to confront a guy who's killed at least a dozen people—if not more." Reports were coming into the precinct from more than a half dozen facilities, all of which had employed Mayfield at one time or other—and all which, coincidentally, had more than their share of patients dying at the time. "You wait for me," he shouted.

Relieved or not, she wasn't about to stand there and

be yelled at. She wanted to be comforted, not upbraided, damn it. "If I'd waited, most likely your grandmother would have been dead by now," she retorted.

"And if I hadn't come in just when I did, *you* would have been dead by now!" he countered, not adding that he realized that he wouldn't have been able to recover from that kind of a blow.

Her eyes narrowed, small slits firing laser beams. "Maybe you would have preferred that," she snapped.

He stared at her incredulously. What the hell was she babbling about?

Tucking away his weapon, he threw up his hands. "All right, it's official. You're crazy."

How dare he say that? Especially since, if she *was* crazy, he and his mercurial behavior had made her that way.

"Well, that's not your problem, is it? Gerald's your killer—he confessed to me—so the case is solved. And from all indications, your grandmother's going to be just fine." Nika had no idea how she knew, she just did. "That means that you don't have to put up with me anymore." She turned away from him, afraid that angry tears were about to come spilling out. She didn't want him thinking that she was crying over him—even though she was.

He grabbed her arm, swinging her around to face him. "Stop making up my mind for me, Veronika. Maybe I want to."

Maybe her anger was shutting down her mind. She had no idea what he was saying. "What? Want to what?"

She was going to make him spell it out, he thought, annoyed. Okay, then if that's what she wanted, that's what she was going to get.

"Maybe I want to put up with you," he shouted back at her. When she widened her eyes like that, he found it hard to maintain his anger. "God damn it, woman, you are the most infuriating person I ever met—and I've never felt as alive as I have when I'm with you."

She looked at him, stunned. "Then why are you shouting at me?"

That was easy to answer. "Because I don't want to feel this way. I want to be numb again. Numb is safe. I do my job and go home. Simple, clean."

She was beginning to understand. Nika's mouth curved. "And I'm messy."

He nodded, finally lowering his voice a little. "Oh so messy."

She paused a second as she rolled the phrase over in her head. "Not exactly the kind of compliment a woman longs to hear." The semi-smile turned into an amused grin. "But I'll take it."

The room began to fill up with people, doctors and nurses who had heard the single gunshot and wanted to know what was going on, as well as several security officers that one of the nurses had summoned.

Processing the scene, they fired questions at Cole and Nika. Cole took the lead and raised his hand, calling for a cessation of noise. It was a toss-up whether it was his commanding voice, or the badge and ID that he held in his hand that quieted the crowd.

Nodding toward the dead orderly, he said, "It looks like this was the last stop for the angel of death."

For another moment, as the words sank in, there was silence. And then a torrent of questions began to engulf him. Cole looked over his shoulder at Nika. "Don't go anywhere—we need to talk."

Her eyes never left his. "About?"

Cole took a breath. Still ignoring the other questions that were being fired at him, he gave Nika an evasive answer. "We just need to talk."

Nika mulled over Cole's nonanswer while he dealt with the security guards and then called for backup. On Nika's end, the wait seemed endless, but finally, the questions, at least for now, were all answered. The orderly's body had been taken to the Medical Examiner to await an autopsy. And Cole's grandmother, who'd slept through everything, was back in her room, still sleeping. After making a cursory report to his superior via his cell phone, Cole went down to his grandmother's room.

Nika was already there.

"You said you wanted to talk," Nika reminded him in response to his surprised look.

"Actually," he admitted with feeling, "I don't. What I really want to do is take you home and make love with you until I drop dead."

"Drop dead," she repeated. "Not exactly the most romantic scenario you could come up with, especially given what we just went through."

"It would be, up until the last part," he pointed out. And then the smile on his lips faded, pushed aside by the serious expression that had come over his features. He took her into his arms, thinking how special that felt— and how lucky he was. And how he'd almost lost it all. "I didn't mean to yell at you before."

An apology. She could forgive him for anything as long as he apologized, she realized. Though she tried to keep a straight face, she failed miserably. "Yes, you did."

"Okay, I did," he admitted, because lying would only

serve him badly in this situation. "But that was only because you put yourself in danger and the consequences of that scared the hell out of me.

"As do the feelings that you've raised. I don't want to feel like this," he confessed, continuing to do what he'd never done before—bare his soul. "I don't want to love you," he insisted, knocking her for a loop when he used the one word she was certain she'd never hear from him. "But I can't seem to block it or turn it off. Or even control it. It's bigger than I am, and stronger."

Her smile felt like it was growing deep roots—instantly. She threaded her arms around his neck. "Why don't you just enjoy it?" she suggested.

"I suppose I could do that," he allowed. "For a while, anyway."

She started to feel her heart sink. "And then?" she pressed. If he intended to leave her someday soon, she needed him to put her on notice. So she'd stop harboring false hopes.

"And then we'll up the ante."

She cocked her head, her eyes on his. "What's that supposed to mean?"

He smiled into her eyes, really smiled. She could feel it penetrating her soul.

"Anything we want it to," he told her. Cole paused, waiting. "What do you think?"

She paused for a second as she selected her words. "I think, Detective Baker, that you and I are going to have a very interesting life." She deliberately refrained from using the word "together." That, she knew in her heart, would come in time. And she could wait.

He ran the back of his hand along her cheek, never taking his eyes off her. "I'm counting on it. You know, of hair slipping from her ponytail and taste her. Apparently he needed to spend a lot less time working and a great deal *more* time recreating with the opposite sex if he could have sudden random fantasies about a woman he wasn't even inclined to like, pretty or not.

"I'm Trace Bowman. You must be new in town."

She didn't answer immediately and he could almost see the wheels turning in her head. Why the hesitancy? And why that little hint of unease he could see clouding the edge of her gaze? His presence was obviously making her uncomfortable and Trace couldn't help wondering why.

"Yes. We've been here a few weeks."

"Well, I'm just up the road about four lots, in the white house with the cedar shake roof, if you or your daughter need anything." He smiled at her as he picked up the last shard of glass and set it on her tray.

Definitely a story there, he thought as she hurried away. He just might need to dig a little into her background to find out why someone with fine clothes and nice jewelry, and who so obviously didn't have experience as a waitress, would be here slinging hash at The Gulch. Was she running away from someone? A bad marriage?

So…Rebecca Parsons. Not Becky. An intriguing woman. It had been a long time since one of those had crossed his path here in Pine Gulch.

Trace won't rest until he finds out Rebecca's secret, but
̶ ̶l he still have that same attraction to her once he does?
Find out in CHRISTMAS IN COLD CREEK.
̶vailable November 2011 from Harlequin® Special Edition®.

Harlequin®

ROMANTIC
SUSPENSE

CARLA CASSIDY

Cowboy's Triplet Trouble

Jake Johnson, the eldest of his triplet brothers, is stunned
when Grace Sinclair turns up on his family's ranch declaring
Jake's younger and irresponsible brother as the father of her
triplets. When Grace's life is threatened, Jake finds himself
fighting a powerful attraction and a need to protect. But as
the threats hit closer to home, Jake begins to wonder
if someone on the ranch is out to kill Grace....

A brand-new Top Secret Deliveries story!

TOP SECRET
DELIVERIES

Available in November wherever books are sold!

www.Harlequin.com

HRS277

after everything that happened to me as a kid, I never thought I would ever feel close to anyone again besides G. And then you came along and somehow burrowed your way in when I wasn't looking. And now, now I can't imagine a day without you."

Warmth spread all through her, right through her fingertips and toes. Her smile was soft, loving. "You know, for a guy who doesn't talk much, that was very touching."

He shrugged, a little self-conscious. "Yeah, well, don't expect this all the time."

Nika's mouth curved as she tried to keep from laughing. *You're mine, Cole Baker, and I'm never letting you go.* "I won't. Oh, and just for the record, I love you, too," she told him softly, lacing her arms around his neck. "Right down to my toes."

"Well, it's about time."

The words, hardly more than a raspy whisper, came from his grandmother. She'd woken up for a span of perhaps thirty seconds.

But when they looked, she was asleep again.

It was just as well, Cole thought. The kiss that followed was far too torrid for a woman her age to witness.

Epilogue

"Mama, this is a happy time. You're not supposed to be crying," Nika chided gently.

She took out the brand-new lace handkerchief that Sasha had given her that morning just before they left for the church and wiped away the lone tear that had insisted on sliding down her mother's cheek.

Paulina pushed aside her daughter's hand. "I am your mother. Do not tell me what I can or cannot do." She indicated the handkerchief still in Nika's hand. "Be putting that away. You are not supposed to be using it. It will not be new if you do," she said crisply in an attempt to maintain her abrupt facade. "And then we will he having to find something else for you to go with the borrowing and the old and blue," she retorted, reciting the age-old articles that each bride was supposed to have in her possession as she walked down the aisle toward her future husband.

Paulina squared her shoulders as she reclaimed her composure. She and her daughter—her beautiful, beautiful daughter—were momentarily alone in the small room reserved for the bride within the church where, a few short minutes from now, her second-born was going to become a married woman.

Her Nika was going to be the wife of a fine young man who had come to Paulina to ask for her daughter's hand. She knew things like that were not done here in this day and age, so the fact that Cole Baker had done this specially pleased her. Her husband, she knew in her heart, would have approved of the match.

"Yes, Mama," Nika said dutifully, then smiled warmly at her mother. "But this really *is* a happy time," she repeated, her voice soft but firm nonetheless.

Paulina raised her chin and sniffed. "I know that," she declared.

Josef heard the exchange between mother and daughter just as he was about to look in on them. He was to give the bride away, and even after having done so five previous times, the responsibility still filled him with pride.

He opened the door wider now. Somewhere in the background could be heard the beginning strains of the song that placed all brides center stage.

"She is your mother," Nika's uncle pointed out. "She is knowing everything."

Nika slanted a quick glance toward her mother. There was a time that would have had her mother's back up—she took offense at every word Nika's uncle and aunt said—but this time Nika saw her mother nod her head, as if she had just been given her due.

"When it is coming to matters concerning my daughters," Paulina said solemnly, "the answer is being yes."

As if on cue, Nika's three sisters came in, all but flooding the room. Alyx took Nika's hands in hers and beamed even as she shook her head. "I can't believe you're getting married ahead of me."

"Only by two weeks," Nika pointed out. "And then we switch positions and I get to be *your* maid of honor."

"Matron of honor," Henryka, the youngest of the foursome, corrected. "You'll be Alyx's *matron* of honor," she repeated, putting a great deal of stress on the word. And then she laughed, her eyes shining as she teased her older sister. "You'll be an old married lady, Nika."

Paulina rallied, defending Nika. It was all well and good for her to be critical of her daughters, but no one else could be, not even her other daughters.

"Which is what you need to become," she informed her youngest, her pointed gaze shifting from Henryka to her third-born. "Both of you."

Looking over her shoulder, Josef raised his voice. "Magda," he called out.

A moment later, his wife appeared in the doorway just behind him. The room had become far too crowded for her to enter.

"Yes, Josef?"

"Please finding a nice escorter—"

"Usher," Magda corrected her husband patiently.

"Usher," he repeated, without missing a beat, "to be taking Paulina to her place of honor now, please."

Nika knew her uncle had phrased it that way to appeal to her mother's need for recognition. It seemed to work. Paulina allowed herself to be drawn from the room by her sister-in-law as Magda took hold of her arm.

"I will see you in the front," Paulina promised Nika, brushing a quick kiss against her daughter's cheek.

With peace once again restored, Nika's sisters all filed dutifully out of the room as the music grew louder.

And then it was just Nika and her uncle.

Josef presented his arm to her and she slipped hers through it. Adrenaline began coursing through her veins. *This is it,* she thought excitedly.

"Your father," Josef told her, his eyes shining with tears it did not become a man to shed, "would be being very proud of you at this moment. As he always was," he added.

"Thank you, Uncle Josef."

He nodded. "All right, now we must be walking. You do not wanting to keep your nice young man waiting."

And with that, she and her uncle walked out into the hall as she took the first steps that would lead her to the rest of her life.

* * * * *

Harlequin

ROMANTIC
SUSPENSE

COMING NEXT MONTH

Available October 25, 2011

#1679 RISKY CHRISTMAS
Holiday Secrets by Jill Sorenson
Kidnapped at Christmas by Jennifer Morey

#1680 MISSING MOTHER-TO-BE
The Kelley Legacy
Elle Kennedy

#1681 COWBOY'S TRIPLET TROUBLE
Top Secret Deliveries
Carla Cassidy

#1682 HIGH-RISK REUNION
Stealth Knights
Gail Barrett

You can find more information on upcoming
Harlequin® titles, free excerpts and more at
www.HarlequinInsideRomance.com.

REQUEST YOUR FREE BOOKS!
2 FREE NOVELS PLUS 2 FREE GIFTS!

◆ **Harlequin**

ROMANTIC
SUSPENSE

Sparked by Danger, Fueled by Passion.

YES! Please send me 2 FREE Harlequin® Romantic Suspense novels and my 2 FREE gifts (gifts are worth about $10). After receiving them, if I don't wish to receive any more books, I can return the shipping statement marked "cancel." If I don't cancel, I will receive 4 brand-new novels every month and be billed just $4.49 per book in the U.S. or $5.24 per book in Canada. That's a saving of at least 14% off the cover price! It's quite a bargain! Shipping and handling is just 50¢ per book in the U.S. and 75¢ per book in Canada.* I understand that accepting the 2 free books and gifts places me under no obligation to buy anything. I can always return a shipment and cancel at any time. Even if I never buy another book, the two free books and gifts are mine to keep forever.

240/340 HDN FEFR

Name	(PLEASE PRINT)

Address		Apt. #

City	State/Prov.	Zip/Postal Code

Signature (if under 18, a parent or guardian must sign)

Mail to the **Reader Service:**
IN U.S.A.: P.O. Box 1867, Buffalo, NY 14240-1867
IN CANADA: P.O. Box 609, Fort Erie, Ontario L2A 5X3

Not valid for current subscribers to Harlequin Romantic Suspense books.

Want to try two free books from another line?
Call 1-800-873-8635 or visit www.ReaderService.com.

* Terms and prices subject to change without notice. Prices do not include applicable taxes. Sales tax applicable in N.Y. Canadian residents will be charged applicable taxes. Offer not valid in Quebec. This offer is limited to one order per household. All orders subject to credit approval. Credit or debit balances in a customer's account(s) may be offset by any other outstanding balance owed by or to the customer. Please allow 4 to 6 weeks for delivery. Offer available while quantities last.

Your Privacy—The Reader Service is committed to protecting your privacy. Our Privacy Policy is available online at www.ReaderService.com or upon request from the Reader Service.

We make a portion of our mailing list available to reputable third parties that offer products we believe may interest you. If you prefer that we not exchange your name with third parties, or if you wish to clarify or modify your communication preferences, please visit us at www.ReaderService.com/consumerschoice or write to us at Reader Service Preference Service, P.O. Box 9062, Buffalo, NY 14269. Include your complete name and address.

Harlequin® Special Edition® is thrilled to present a new installment in USA TODAY bestselling author RaeAnne Thayne's reader-favorite miniseries, THE COWBOYS OF COLD CREEK.

Join the excitement as we meet the Bowmans—four siblings who lost their parents but keep family ties alive in Pine Gulch. First up is Trace. Only two things get under this rugged lawman's skin: beautiful women and secrets. And in Rebecca Parsons, he finds both!

Read on for a sneak peek of CHRISTMAS IN COLD CREEK. Available November 2011 from Harlequin® Special Edition®.

On impulse, he unfolded himself from the bar stool. "Need a hand?"

"Thank you! I…" She lifted her gaze from the floor to his jeans and then raised her eyes. When she identified him her hazel eyes turned from grateful to unfriendly and cold, as if he'd somehow thrown the broken glasses at her head.

He also thought he saw a glimmer of panic in those interesting depths, which instantly stirred his curiosity like cream swirling through coffee.

"I've got it, Officer. Thank you." Her voice was several degrees colder than the whirl of sleet outside the windows.

Despite her protests, he knelt down beside her and began to pick up shards of broken glass. "No problem. Those trays can be slippery."

This close, he picked up the scent of her, something fresh and flowery that made him think of a mountain meadow on a July afternoon. She had a soft, lush mouth and for one brief, insane moment, he wanted to push aside that stray lock